P9-CBC-403

The Gift

G·K
Hall
&C.

*Also by Danielle Steel
in Large Print:*

Mixed Blessings
Jewels
No Greater Love
Heartbeat
Message from Nam
Daddy
Star
Wanderlust
Secrets
Family Album
Full Circle
Changes
Thurston House
Crossings
Once in a Lifetime
Remembrance
The Ring

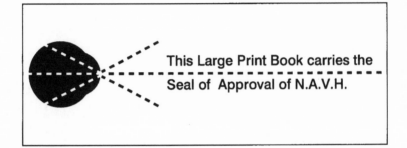

This Large Print Book carries the
Seal of Approval of N.A.V.H.

DANIELLE STEEL

The Gift

G.K. Hall & Co. • Thorndike, Maine

DEER PARK PUBLIC LIBRARY
44 LAKE AVENUE
DEER PARK, NY 11729

Copyright © 1994 by Danielle Steel

All rights reserved.

Published in 1998 by arrangement with Delacorte Press, an imprint of Dell Publishing, a division of Bantam Doubleday Dell Publishing Group, Inc.

G.K. Hall Large Print Core Series.

The text of this Large Print edition is unabridged.
Other aspects of the book may vary from the original edition.

Set in 16 pt. Plantin by Minnie B. Raven.

Printed in the United States on permanent paper. 27,95

Library of Congress Cataloging in Publication Data

Steel, Danielle.
 The gift / Danielle Steel.
  p. cm.
 ISBN 0-7838-0180-7 (lg. print : hc : alk. paper)
 1. Large type books. I. Title.
[PS3569.T33828G5 1998]
813'.54—dc21   98-17699

To the gifts in my life,
my husband, John, and all of my children,
and to the angels who have passed
through my life, quickly or over time,
and the blessings they've brought me.
With all my love,

d.s.

Chapter One

Annie Whittaker loved everything about Christmas. She loved the weather, and the trees, brightly lit on everyone's front lawn, and the Santas outlined in lights on the roofs of people's houses. She loved the carols, and waiting for Santa Claus to come, going skating and drinking hot chocolate afterwards, and stringing popcorn with her mother and sitting wide-eyed afterwards looking at how beautiful their Christmas tree was, all lit up. Her mother just let her sit there in the glow of it, her five-year-old face filled with wonder.

Elizabeth Whittaker was forty-one when Annie was born and she came as a surprise. Elizabeth had long since given up the dream of having another baby. They had tried for years before, Tommy was ten by then, and they had finally made their peace with having only one child. Tommy was a great kid, and Liz and John had always felt lucky. He played football, and baseball with the Little League, and he was the star of the ice hockey team every winter. He was a good boy, and he did everything he was supposed to do, he did well in school, was loving to them, and still there was enough mischief in him to reassure them that he was normal. He was by no means the perfect child, but he was a good boy. He had blond hair like Liz, and sharp blue eyes like his father. He had a good sense of humor and a fine mind, and after the initial shock, he seemed to adjust to the idea of having a baby sister.

And for the past five and a half years, since she'd been born, he thought the sun rose and set on Annie. She was a wispy little thing with a big grin, and a giggle that rang out in the house every time she and Tommy were together. She waited anxiously for him to come home from school every day, and then they sat eating cookies and drinking milk in the kitchen. Liz had changed to substitute teaching, instead of working full-time after Annie was born. She said she wanted to enjoy every minute of her last baby. And she had. They were together constantly.

Liz even found time to do volunteer work at the nursery school for two years, and now she helped with the art program at the kindergarten that Annie attended. They baked cookies and bread and biscuits together in the afternoons, or Liz read to her for hours as they sat together in the big cozy kitchen. Their lives were a warm place, where all four of them felt safe from the kinds of things that happened to other people. And John took good care of them. He ran the state's largest wholesale produce business, and he earned a decent living for all of them. He had done well early on, it had been his father and grandfather's business before him. They had a handsome house in the better part of town.

They were by no means rich, but they were safe from the cold winds of change that touched farmers and people in businesses that were often adversely affected by trends and fashion. Everyone needed good food, and John Whittaker had always provided it for them. He was a warm, caring man, and he hoped that Tommy would come into the business one day too. But first, he wanted him to go to college. And Annie too, he wanted her to be just as smart and well educated as her mother. Annie wanted to be a teacher, just like her mom, but John dreamed of her being a doctor or a lawyer. For 1952, these were strong dreams, but John had already saved a handsome sum for Annie's education. He'd put Tommy's college money away several years before, so financially they were both well on their way toward college. He was a man who believed in dreams. He always said there was nothing you couldn't do if you wanted it bad enough, and were willing to work hard enough to get it. And he had always been a willing worker. And Liz had always been a great help to him, but he was happy to let her stay home now. He loved coming home in the late afternoons, to find her cuddled up with Annie, or watch the two of them playing dolls in Annie's room. It warmed his heart just to see them. He was forty-nine years old and a happy man. He had a wonderful wife, and two terrific children.

"Where is everyone?" he called that afternoon as he came in, brushing the snow and ice off his hat and coat, and pushing the dog away, as she wagged her tail and slid around in the puddles he'd made on the floor around him. She was a big Irish setter they had named Bess, after the president's wife. Liz had tried to argue at first that it was a disrespect to Mrs. Truman, but the name seemed to suit her, and it had stuck, and no one seemed to remember how she'd gotten her name now.

"We're back here," Liz called out, and John walked into the living room to find them hanging gingerbread men on the tree. They had decorated them all afternoon, and Annie had made paper chains while the cookies were in the oven.

"Hi, Daddy, isn't it beautiful?"

"It is." He smiled down at her, and then lifted her into his arms with ease. He was a powerful man, with the Irish coloring of his forebears. He had black hair, even now, a year shy of fifty. And brilliant blue eyes, which he had bestowed on both of his children. And in spite of her blond hair, Liz's eyes were a soft brown, sometimes almost hazel. But Annie's hair was almost white it was so fair. And as she smiled into her father's eyes and rubbed her tiny nose playfully against his, she looked like an angel. He set her down gently next to him, and then reached up to kiss his wife, as an affectionate look passed between them.

"How was your day?" she asked warmly. They had been married for twenty-two years, and most of the time, when life's petty aggravations weren't nibbling at them, they seemed more in love than ever. They had married two years after Liz graduated from college. She'd already been a teacher by then, and it had taken seven years for Tommy to appear. They had almost given up hope and old Dr. Thompson had never really figured out why she either couldn't get, or stay, pregnant. She had had three miscarriages before Tommy was born, and it seemed like a miracle to them when he finally came. And even more so when Annie was born ten years later. They admitted easily that they were blessed, and the children gave them all the joy that they had hoped and expected.

"I got the oranges in from Florida today," John said as he sat down and picked up his pipe. There was a fire in the fireplace, and the house smelled of gingerbread and popcorn. "I'll bring some home tomorrow."

"I love oranges!" Annie clapped her hands, and then climbed on his lap, while Bess put both of her paws up on John's knees and tried to join them. John pushed the dog away gently, and Liz came down the ladder to kiss him again and offer him a glass of hot cider.

"Sounds too good to turn down." He smiled, and then followed her into the kitchen a moment later, silently admiring her trim figure. He was holding Annie's hand, and it was only moments after when the front door slammed, and Tommy came in, with a pink nose and bright red cheeks, carrying his ice skates.

"Mmm . . . smells good . . . hi, Mom . . . hi, Dad . . . hey, squirt, what did you do today? Eat all of your mom's cookies?" He ruffled her hair and gave her a squeeze, getting her face wet with his own. It was freezing outside, and snowing harder every moment.

"I *made* the cookies with Mommy . . . and I only ate four of them," she said meticulously as they laughed. She was so cute she was hard for anyone to resist, least of all her big brother, or her doting parents. But she wasn't spoiled. She was just well loved, and it showed in the ease with which she faced the world and met every challenge. She liked everyone, loved to laugh, loved playing games, loved running in the wind with her hair flying out behind her. She loved to play with Bess . . . but better yet her older brother. She looked up at him adoringly now, taking in the well-worn ice skates. "Can we go skating tomorrow, Tommy?" There was a pond nearby, and he took her there often on Saturday mornings.

"If it stops snowing by then. If this keeps up, you won't even be able to find the pond," he said, munching on one of his mother's delicious cookies. They were mouthwatering, and they were all Tommy could think of, as his mother carefully took off her apron. She wore a neat blouse and a full gray skirt, and it always pleased John to notice that she still had the figure she'd had when he first met her in high school. She'd been a freshman when he was a senior, and for a long time it had embarrassed him to admit that he was in love with a girl so young, but eventually everyone had figured it out. They teased them at first, but after a while, everyone took them for granted. He'd gone to work for his father the following year, and she had spent another seven years finishing high school and college, and then two more working as a teacher. He had waited a long time for her, but he never doubted for a minute that it was worth it. Everything they had ever really wanted or cared about had come to them slowly, like their children. But all the good things in their lives had been worth the wait. They were happy now. They had everything they had always wanted.

"I've got a game tomorrow afternoon," Tommy mentioned casually as he gobbled up two more cookies.

"The day before Christmas Eve?" his mother asked, surprised. "You'd think people would have other things to do." They always went to his games, unless something really major happened to prevent it. John had played ice hockey too, and football. He had loved it too. Liz was a little less sure, she didn't want Tommy to get injured. A couple of the boys had lost teeth in ice hockey games over the years, but Tommy was careful, and pretty lucky. No broken bones, no major injuries, just a lot of sprains and bruises, which his father claimed were all part of the fun.

"He's a boy for heaven's sake, you can't wrap

him up in cotton wool forever." But secretly she admitted to herself sometimes that she would have liked to. Her children were so precious to her, she never wanted anything bad to happen to them, or to John. She was a woman who cherished her blessings.

"Was today your last day of school before Christmas?" Annie asked him with interest, and he nodded with a grin. He had lots of plans for the holidays, many of which included a girl named Emily he'd had his eye on since Thanksgiving. She had just moved to Grinnell that year. Her mom was a nurse and her father was a doctor. They had moved from Chicago, and she was pretty cute. Cute enough for Tommy to ask her to several of his hockey games. But he had gone no further than that yet. He was going to ask her to go to the movies with him the following week, and maybe even do something with him on New Year's Eve, but he hadn't gotten up the courage yet to ask her.

Annie knew he liked Emily too. She had seen him staring at Emily one day when they had gone to the pond, and run into her. She was there skating with some of her friends and one of her sisters. Annie thought she was okay, but she couldn't see why Tommy was that crazy about her. She had long, shiny dark hair, and she was a pretty fair skater. But she didn't say much to him, she just kept looking over at them, and then as they left, she made a big fuss over Annie.

"She just did that because she likes you," she explained matter-of-factly, as they walked home, with Tommy carrying Annie's ice skates.

"What makes you say that?" he asked, trying to sound cool, but managing to look both awkward and nervous.

"She kept looking at you goo-goo-eyed all the time when you were skating." Annie flung her long blond hair knowingly over her shoulder.

"What do you mean, 'goo-goo-eyed'?"

"You know what I mean. You know, she's crazy about you. That's why she was nice to me. She has a little sister too, and she's never that nice to her. I told you, she likes you."

"You know too much, Annie Whittaker. Aren't you supposed to be playing with dolls or something?" He tried to look unaffected by what she'd said, and then reminded himself of how dumb it was to worry about how he looked to his five-and-a-half-year-old sister.

"You really like her, don't you?" She was needling him then, and giggled as she asked him.

"Why don't you mind your own business?" He sounded sharp with her, which was rare, and Annie didn't pay any attention.

"I think her older sister is a lot cuter."

"I'll keep that in mind, in case I ever want to go out with a senior."

"What's wrong with seniors?" Annie looked baffled by the distinction.

"Nothing. Except that she's seventeen years old," he explained, and Annie nodded wisely.

"That's too old. I guess Emily is okay then."

"Thank you."

"You're welcome," she said seriously, as they reached home, and went inside to drink hot chocolate and get warm. In spite of her comments about the girls in his life, he really liked being with her. Annie always made him feel enormously loved, and extremely important. She worshiped him, and she made no bones about it. She adored him. And he loved her just as much.

She sat on his lap that night before she went to bed, and he read her her favorite stories. He read the shortest one to her twice, and then their mother took her off to bed, and he sat and chatted with his father. They talked about Eisenhower's election the month before, and the changes it might bring. And then they talked, as they always did, about the business. His father wanted him to get a degree in agriculture, with a minor in economics. They believed in basic, but important things, like family, and kids, and the sanctity of marriage, and honesty, and being helpful to their friends. They were much loved and respected in the community. And people always said about John Whittaker that he was a good husband, a fine man, and a fair employer.

Tommy went off with some of his friends that night. The weather was so bad he didn't even ask to borrow the car, he just walked to his closest friend, and then came home at eleven-thirty. They never had to worry about him. He'd sown

one or two wild oats by fifteen, all of which con-
sisted of two instances of drinking too much
beer and throwing up in the car when his father
brought him home. The Whittakers hadn't been
pleased, but they hadn't gone crazy about it
either. He was a good boy, and they knew that
all kids did those things. John had done them
too, and a few worse, especially while Liz had
been away at college. She teased him about it
sometimes, and he insisted that he had been a
model of virtuous behavior, to which she raised
an eyebrow, and then usually kissed him.

They went to bed early that night too, and
the next morning, as they looked out their win-
dows, it looked like a Christmas card. Everything was white and beautiful, and by eight-
thirty that morning Annie had Tommy outside
with her, helping her build a snowman. She used
Tommy's favorite hockey cap too, and he explained that he was going to have to "borrow"
it that afternoon for his game, and Annie said
she'd have to let him know if he could use it.
He tossed her into the snow then, and they lay
there, on their backs, waving their arms and legs,
making "angels."

They all went to Tommy's game that afternoon, and even though his team lost, he was in
good spirits afterwards. Emily had come to see
him too, although she was surrounded by a
group of friends, and claimed that they had
wanted to come, and she had just "happened"
to join them. She was wearing a plaid skirt and

17

saddle shoes, and her long dark hair was in a ponytail down her back, and Annie said she was wearing makeup.

"How do you know?" He looked surprised and amused as the whole family left the skating rink at school and walked home together. Emily had already left with her gaggle of giggling girl-friends.

"I wear Mom's makeup sometimes," Annie said matter-of-factly, and both men grinned and looked down at the little elf walking beside them.

"Mom doesn't wear makeup," Tommy said just as firmly.

"Yes, she does. She wears powder and rouge, and sometimes she wears lipstick."

"She does?" Tommy looked surprised. His mother was nice-looking, he knew, but he never suspected that there was any artifice involved, or that she actually wore makeup.

"Sometimes she wears black stuff on her eye-lashes too, but it makes you cry if you use it," Annie explained, and Liz laughed.

"It makes me cry too, that's why I never wear it."

They talked about the game then, and other things, and Tommy went out with his friends again, and a classmate of his came to baby-sit for Annie that night, so her parents could go to a Christmas party at a neighbor's house.

They were back home by ten o'clock, and in bed by midnight, and Annie was sound asleep in her bed when they came home. But she was

18

up at dawn the next morning, and wildly excited about Christmas. It was Christmas Eve, and all she could think of was what she had asked Santa Claus for. She wanted a Madame Alexander doll desperately, and she wasn't at all sure she would get one. And she wanted a new sled too, and a bicycle, but she knew it would be better to get the bicycle in the spring, on her birthday.

There seemed to be a thousand things to do that day too, a myriad of preparations for Christmas. They were expecting some friends to visit the following afternoon, and her mother was doing some last-minute baking. And they'd be going to midnight mass that night. It was a ritual Annie loved, although she didn't really understand it. But she loved going to church with them, late at night, and being sandwiched between her parents in the warm church, dozing off, as she listened to the hymns and smelled the incense. There was a beautiful manger with all the animals surrounding Joseph and Mary. And at midnight, they put the baby in the manger, too. She loved looking for it before they left the church, and seeing baby Jesus there with his mother.

"Just like you and me, huh Mom?" she asked, nestling close to Liz, as her mother bent down to kiss her.

"Just like us," Liz said gently, counting her blessings again. "I love you, Annie."

"I love you too," Annie whispered.

She went to the service with them that night,

as she always did, and fell asleep as she sat comfortably between her parents. It was so cozy and pleasant there. The church was warm, and the music seemed to lull her to sleep. She didn't even wake up for the procession. But she checked for baby Jesus in the manger, as she always did, on the way out, and he was there. She smiled when she saw the little statue, and then looked up at her mother and squeezed her hand. Liz felt tears in her eyes as she looked at her. Annie was like a special gift to them, sent just to bring them joy and warmth and laughter.

It was after one in the morning when they got home that night, and Annie seemed more asleep than awake when they put her to bed. And by the time Tommy went in to kiss her, she was sound asleep and gently snoring. He thought she felt kind of hot, when he kissed her head, but he didn't think much of it. He didn't even bother to tell his mom. She looked so peaceful that he didn't think anything was wrong.

But she slept late on Christmas morning for the first time and she seemed a little dazed when she woke up. Liz had put out the plate of carrots and salt for the reindeer, and the cookies for Santa the night before because Annie had been too sleepy to do it. But Annie remembered to check to see what they'd eaten when she woke up. She was a little sleepier than usual, and she said she had a headache, but she didn't have a cold, and Liz thought maybe she was coming down with a mild case of influenza. It had been so bitter cold lately, and she might have gotten a chill playing in the snow with Tommy two days before. But by lunchtime she seemed fine. And she was elated over the Madame Alexander doll Santa had brought her, and the other toys, and the new sled. She went out with Tommy and played for an hour, and when she came in for hot chocolate that afternoon her cheeks were bright red and she looked very healthy.

"So, Princess," her father smiled happily at her, puffing on his pipe. Liz had given him a beautiful new one from Holland, and a hand-carved rack for all his old ones. "Was Santa Claus good to you?"

"The best." She grinned. "My new dolly is so pretty, Daddy." She smiled up at him as though she almost knew who had given it to her, but of course she didn't. They all worked hard to keep the myth going for her, although a few of her friends knew. But Liz insisted that Santa Claus comes to all good children, and even some not so good ones, in the hope that they'd get better. But there was no question as to which kind Annie was. She was the best, to them, and to everyone who knew her.

They had friends in that afternoon, three families who lived nearby and two of John's managers with their wives and children. The house was quickly filled with laughter and games. There were a few young people Tommy's age too, and he showed them his new fishing rod. He could hardly wait for the spring to use it.

It was a warm, enjoyable afternoon, and they had a quiet dinner that night, after everyone had gone. Liz had made turkey soup, and they ate leftovers from lunch, and some of the goodies people had brought them.

"I don't think I'll be able to eat again for a month," John said, stretching back in his chair, as his wife smiled, and then noticed that Annie looked kind of pale and glassy-eyed, and there were two bright spots on her cheeks, which looked like the rouge she liked to play with.

"Have you been into my makeup again?" Liz asked with a mild look of concern mixed with amusement.

"No . . . it went into the snow . . . and then I . . ." She seemed to be confused, and then looked up at Liz, surprised, as though she wasn't sure herself what she had just said, and it scared her.

"Are you okay, sweetheart?" Liz leaned over to gently touch her forehead, and it was blazing. She had seemed happy enough that afternoon, she had played with her new doll and her friends, and she seemed to be running through the living room or the kitchen every time Liz saw her. "Do you feel sick?"

"Sort of." Annie shrugged, and looked suddenly very little as she said it, and Liz pulled her onto her lap and held her. But just holding her there, she could tell that Annie was running a fever. She put a hand on her head again and thought about calling the doctor.

"I hate to bother him on Christmas night," Liz said pensively. And it was so bitter cold again. There was a storm coming in from the north, and they said it would be snowing again before morning.

"She'll be fine after a good night's sleep," John said calmly. He was less of a worrier than Liz by nature. "It's just too much excitement for one small person." They'd all been wound up for days, with seeing friends, and Tommy's game, and Christmas Eve, and all the preparations for Christmas. And Liz decided he was probably right. It was a lot for one little girl to handle. "How about riding to bed on Daddy's shoulders?" She liked the idea, but when he tried to lift her up, she called out sharply and said her neck hurt.

"What do you suppose that is?" Liz asked, as he came out of Annie's bedroom.

"Just a cold. Everyone at work's had one for weeks, and I'm sure all the kids have them at school. She'll be fine," he reassured his wife, with a pat on the shoulder. And she knew he was right, but she always worried about things like polio and tuberculosis. "She's fine," John said to Liz again, knowing how inclined she was to be overly concerned. "I promise."

She went to kiss Annie herself then, and felt better when she saw her. Her eyes were bright, and although her head was hot, and she was still pale, she seemed completely coherent. She was probably just tired and overexcited. And he was right. She had a cold, or a little flu bug.

"You sleep tight, and if you feel sick, come and get us," Liz told her as she tucked her tightly into bed and kissed her. "I love you very, very much, sweetheart . . . and thank you for the beautiful picture you made me and Daddy for Christmas." She had made John an ashtray too, for his pipe, and painted it bright green, which she said was his favorite color.

Annie seemed to fall asleep almost before Liz left the room. And after she finished the dishes, she went back and checked her. Annie was even hotter by then, and she was stirring and moaning in her sleep, but she didn't wake up when Liz touched her. It was ten o'clock, and Liz decided it was worthwhile just calling the doctor.

He was at home, and she explained that Annie had a fever. She didn't want to risk waking her up by taking it, but she had had a hundred and one when she went to bed, which wasn't dangerous. She mentioned the stiff neck, and he said that aches and pains weren't unusual with the flu. He agreed with John that she was probably just overtired and had caught a cold over the weekend.

"Bring her in tomorrow morning, Liz, if the fever's gone, or I'll come by to see her. Just give me a call when she wakes up. But she'll be fine. I've got a couple of dozen of those bad colds with fevers. They don't amount to much, but they're pretty miserable while they last. Keep her warm, the fever might even break before morning."

24

"Thanks so much, Walt." Walter Stone had been their family doctor since before Tommy was born, and he was a good friend. As always, she'd felt reassured the minute she'd called him. And he was right. It was obviously nothing.

She and John sat in the living room for a long time that night, talking about their friends, their lives, their kids, how lucky they were, how many years had passed since they'd first met, and how well filled they had been. It was a time for taking stock and being grateful.

She checked on Annie again before they went to bed, and she seemed no warmer, and in fact, she seemed a little less restless. She lay very still, breathing softly. Bess, the dog, lay near the foot of her bed, as she often did. And neither child, nor dog, stirred as Liz left the room and went back to her own bedroom.

"How is she?" John asked, as he slid into bed.

"She's fine," Liz smiled. "I know. I worry too much. I can't help it."

"It's part of why I love you. You take such good care of all of us. I don't know what I ever did to get so lucky."

"Just smart I guess, to snap me up when I was fourteen." She had never known or loved another man before or since. And in the thirty-two years since she'd known him, her love for him had grown to passion.

"You don't look much older than fourteen now, you know," he said almost shyly, and pulled her gently onto the bed with him. She

25

came easily to him, and he slowly unbuttoned her blouse, as she slid off the velvet skirt she'd worn for Christmas. "I love you, Liz," he whispered into her neck, as she felt her desire for him mount, and his hands run smoothly over her naked shoulders to her waiting breasts and his lips came down on hers firmly.

They lay together for a long time, and then at last they slept, sated and pleased. Theirs was a life filled with the good things they had built and found over the years. Theirs was a love they both respected and cherished. And Liz was thinking about him as she drifted off to sleep in his arms. He held her close to him, as he lay just behind her, his arms tight around her waist, his knees just behind hers, her bottom cupped by his body, his face nestled in her fine blond hair, and they slept together peacefully until morning.

She checked on Annie again as soon as she woke up the next day. Liz was still wrapping her dressing gown around her as she tied it, and entered Annie's room, and saw her there, still sleeping. She didn't look sick, but as soon as Liz approached, she saw that she was deathly pale, and barely breathing. Liz's heart pounded suddenly as she shook her a little bit, and waited for her to stir, but there was only a soft groan, and she didn't wake to her mother's touch, not even when Liz shook her hard, and started to shout her name. Tommy heard her before John and came running in to see what had happened.

"What's wrong, Mom?" It was as though he had sensed something the moment he heard her. He still had his pajamas on, he looked half asleep and his hair was tousled.

"I don't know. Tell Dad to call Dr. Stone. I can't wake Annie up." She was starting to cry as she said it. She put her face down next to her child's, and she could feel her breathing, but Annie was unconscious, and she could tell instantly that her fever had skyrocketed since the night before. Liz didn't even dare leave her long enough to get the thermometer in the bathroom. "Hurry!" she called after his retreating form, and then she tried sitting her up. She stirred a little this time, and there was a little muffled cry, but she didn't speak or open her eyes, or seem to wake at all. She seemed not to know what was happening around her, and Liz just sat there and held her, crying softly. "Please, baby . . . please wake up . . . come on . . . I love you . . . Annie, please . . ." She was crying when John hurried into the room a moment later, with Tommy right behind him.

"Walt said he'll be right over. What happened?" He looked frightened too, although he didn't like to admit to Liz that he was worried. And Tommy was crying softly just behind his father's shoulder.

"I don't know . . . I think she has an awful fever . . . I can't wake her up . . . oh God . . . oh John . . . please . . ." She was sobbing, clutching her little girl, holding her as she sat there,

27

rocking her, but this time Annie didn't even moan. She lay lifeless in her mother's arms, while her whole family watched her.

"She'll be all right. Kids get things like this, and then two hours later, they're fine. You know that." John tried to hide the fact that he was panicked.

"Don't tell me what I know. I know she's very sick, that's all I know," Liz snapped nervously at her husband.

"Walt said he'd take her to the hospital if he had to." But it was already obvious to all of them that he would. "Why don't you get dressed," John suggested gently. "I'll watch her."

"I'm not leaving her," Liz said firmly. She laid Annie down on the bed again, and smoothed her hair, as Tommy watched his sister in terror. She looked almost dead she was so white, and unless you looked very carefully, you couldn't tell if she was breathing. It was hard to believe that she would wake up at any moment, giggling and laughing, and yet he wanted to believe that that could still happen.

"How did she get so sick so fast? She was fine last night," Tommy said, looking shocked and confused.

"She was sick, but I thought it was nothing." Liz glared suddenly at John, as though it was his fault that she hadn't asked the doctor to come the night before. It sickened her now to think that they had made love while Annie was slipping into unconsciousness in her bedroom. "I should have made Walt come last night."

"You couldn't know she'd be like this," John reassured her, and she said nothing.

And then they heard him knocking at the door. John ran to open it and let the doctor in. It was bitter cold outside, and the promised storm had come. It was snowing, and the world outside looked as bleak as the one in Annie's bedroom.

"What happened?" the doctor was asking John as he strode quickly to her bedroom.

"I don't know. Liz says her fever has gone sky-high, and we can't seem to wake her up." They were in the doorway by then, and barely acknowledging Liz or their son, he took two steps to Annie's bed, felt her, tried to move her head, and checked her pupils. He listened to her chest, and checked some of her reflexes in total silence, and then he turned and looked at them with a pained expression.

"I'd like to take her to the hospital and do a spinal tap on her, I think it's meningitis."

"Oh my God." Liz wasn't sure what the implications of it were, but she was sure that was not good news, especially given the way Annie was looking. "Will she be all right?" Liz barely whispered the words as she clutched John's arm, and Tommy, crying in the doorway, watching the sister he adored, was momentarily forgotten. Liz could hear her heart pounding as she waited for the doctor's answer. He had been their friend for so long, he had even gone to school with them, but now he seemed like the enemy, as he assessed Annie's fate and told them.

"I don't know," he said honestly. "She's a very sick little girl. I'd like to get her into the hospital right away. Can one of you come with me?"

"We both will," John said firmly. "Just give us a second to get dressed. Tommy, you stay with the doctor and Annie."

"I . . . Dad . . ." He was choking on his words, the tears coming faster than he could stop them. "I want to come too . . . I . . . have to be there . . ." John was about to argue with him, and then nodded. He understood. He knew what she meant to him, to all of them. They couldn't lose her.

"Go get dressed." And then he turned to the doctor. "We'll be ready in a minute."

In their bedroom, Liz was already pulling on her clothes. She had already put on her underwear and a bra, and she had put on her girdle and stockings. She stepped into an old skirt, a pair of boots, and pulled on a sweater, ran a comb through her hair, grabbed her bag and coat, and ran back to Annie's bedroom.

"How is she?" she asked breathlessly as she hurried into the room.

"No change," the doctor said quietly. He had been checking her vital signs constantly. Her blood pressure was way down, her pulse was weak, and she was slipping even further into a coma. He wanted her in the hospital immediately, but he also knew only too well, that even in the hospital there was very little they could do for meningitis.

John appeared dressed haphazardly a moment later too, and Tommy appeared in his hockey uniform. It was the first thing that had fallen into his hands in his closet.

"Let's go," John said, scooping Annie up off the bed, as Liz wrapped her in two heavy blankets. The little head was so hot it almost felt like a lightbulb. It was dry and parched and her lips seemed faintly blue. They ran to the doctor's car and John got into the backseat holding Annie. Liz slipped in beside him, as Tommy got into the front seat next to the doctor. Annie stirred for a moment again then, but she never made another sound as they drove to the hospital, and the entire group was silent. Liz kept looking down at her, and smoothing the blond hair back from her face. She kissed her forehead once or twice, and the white heat of her child's head horrified her as her lips touched her.

John carried her into the emergency room, and the nurses were waiting for them. Walt had called before they left the house, and Liz stood next to Annie, holding her hand and shaking as they did the spinal tap. They had wanted her to leave the room, but she had refused to leave her daughter.

"I'm staying right here with her," she said fiercely. The nurses exchanged a glance, and the doctor nodded.

31

And by the end of the afternoon, they knew for a fact what he had suspected. Annie had meningitis. Her fever had gone up still further by that afternoon. She had a hundred and six point nine, and none of their efforts to lower it had had any effect whatsoever. She lay in the hospital bed, in the children's ward, with the curtain pulled around her, and her parents and brother watching her, and she moaned softly from time to time but she never woke or stirred. And when the doctor checked her, her neck was completely rigid. He knew she couldn't last for long unless the fever broke, or she regained consciousness, but there was nothing they could do to bring her back or battle the disease for her. It was all in the hands of the fates. She had come to them as a gift five and a half years before, and had brought them nothing but love and joy, and now they could do nothing to stop the gift from being taken from them, except pray and hope, and beg her not to leave them. But she seemed to hear nothing at all, as her mother stood next to her, and kissed her face, and stroked her blazing little hand. John and Tommy alternately held the other hand, and then left to walk in the hall and cry. None of them had ever felt as helpless. But it was Liz who refused to let go, or give up without a fight. She felt as though leaving her for a moment might lose the battle. She wasn't going to let her slip silently into the dark, she was going to cling to her, and hold on, and fight to keep her.

"We love you, baby . . . we all love you so much . . . Daddy, and Tommy, and I . . . you have to wake up . . . you have to open your eyes . . . come on, baby . . . come on . . . I know you can do it. You're going to be fine. . . . This is just a silly bug trying to make you sick and we won't let it, will we? . . . come on, Annie . . . come on, baby . . . please. . . ." She talked to her tirelessly for hours, and even late that afternoon, she refused to leave her. She finally accepted a chair, and sat down, still holding Annie's hand, and sometimes she sat silently, and sometimes she talked to her, and sometimes John had to leave because he couldn't bear it. By dinnertime, the nurses took Tommy away because he was so beside himself he couldn't take it anymore, watching his mother beg her to live, and his little sister whom he loved so much, still so lifeless. He could see what it was doing to his dad, and to his mom, and it was all too much for him. He just stood there and sobbed, and Liz didn't have the strength to comfort him too. She held him for a moment, and then the nurses led him away. Annie needed her too much. Liz couldn't leave her to go to Tommy. She would have to talk to him later.

He had been gone for about an hour, when Annie let out a little soft moan, and then her eyelashes seemed to flutter. For a minute it looked as though she might open her eyes, and then she didn't. Instead, she moaned again, but this time she gently squeezed her mother's hand,

and then as though she'd simply been asleep all day, she opened her eyes and looked at her mommy.

"Annie?" Liz said in a whisper, totally stunned by what she was seeing. She signaled John to come closer to them. He had come back into the room and was standing near the door. "Hi, baby . . . Daddy and I are right here, and we love you so much." Her father had reached her bedside by then, and each of them stood on one side of her pillow. She couldn't move her head toward either of them, but it was obvious that she could see them clearly. She looked sleepy, and she closed her eyes for an instant again, and then opened them slowly, and smiled.

"I love you," she said so softly they could hardly hear her. "Tommy? . . ."

"He's here too." There were rivers of tears pouring down Liz's face as she answered her, and she gently kissed her forehead as John cried too, no longer even embarrassed for her to see it. They loved her so much. He would do anything to get her to come through this.

"Love Tommy . . ." she said softly again. ". . . love you . . ." and then she smiled clearly, looking more beautiful and more perfect than ever. She looked like the perfect child, lying there, so blond with big blue eyes, and the little round cheeks they all loved to kiss. She was smiling at them, as though she knew a secret they didn't. Tommy came into the room then, and he saw her too. She looked toward the foot of her bed and smiled right at him. He thought it meant that she was better again, and he began to cry with relief that they wouldn't lose her. And then, seeming to take them all in with her words, she said simply, ". . . thank you . . ." in the smallest of whispers. She closed her eyes then, with a smile, and a moment later she was sleeping, exhausted by her efforts. Tommy was rejoicing at what he'd seen as he left the room again, but Liz knew different. She sensed that something was wrong, that this didn't mean what it appeared to. And as she watched her, she could sense her drift away. The gift that she had been was gone again. It was being taken from them. They had had her for so brief a time, it seemed like barely more than moments. Liz sat holding her hand, and watching her, as John came and went. Tommy was asleep in a chair in the hallway by then. And it was almost midnight when she finally left them. She never opened her eyes again. She never woke. She had said what she had needed to tell them . . . she had told each of them how much she'd loved them . . . she had even thanked them . . . thank you . . . for five beautiful years . . . five tiny short years . . . thank you for this golden little life given to us so briefly. Liz and John were with her when she died, each one holding a hand, not so much to hold her back, but to thank her too for all she gave them. They knew by then that there would be no keeping her from leaving them, they simply wanted to be there when she left them.

"I love you," Liz whispered for a last time, as she breathed the smallest of last breaths. . . . "I love you. . . ." It was only an echo. She had left them on angel wings. The gift had been taken from them. Annie Whittaker was a spirit. And her brother slept on in the hall, remembering her . . . thinking of her . . . loving her . . . just as they all had . . . remembering only days before when they had pretended to be angels in the snow, and now, she truly was one.

Chapter Two

The funeral was an agony of pain and tenderness, the kind of stuff of which mothers' nightmares are made. It was two days before New Year's Eve, and all their friends came, children, parents, her teachers from kindergarten and nursery school, John's associates and employees, and the teachers Liz had taught with. Walter Stone was there too. He told them in a quiet aside that he reproached himself for not having come out the night Liz called. He had assumed it was only a flu or a cold, and he shouldn't have made that assumption. He admitted too, that even if he had come, he wouldn't have been able to change anything. The statistics on meningitis were in almost every instance devastating in young children. Liz and John kindly urged him not to blame himself, and yet Liz blamed herself for not asking him to come out to the house that night, and John blamed himself equally for telling Liz it was nothing. Both hated themselves for having made love while she slipped into a coma in her bed. And Tommy was unsure why he felt that way, but he blamed himself for her death too. He should have been able to make a difference. But none of them had.

Annie had been, as the priest said that day, a

gift to them for a brief time, a little angel on loan to them from God — a little friend come to teach them love and bring them closer together. And she had. Each person who sat there remembered the impish smile, the big blue eyes, the shining little face that made everyone laugh or smile, or love her. There was no doubt in anyone's mind that she had come to them as a gift of love. The question was how they would live on now, without her. It seemed to all of them as though the death of a child stands as a reproach for all one's sins, and a reminder of all one stands to lose in life at any moment. It is the loss of everything, of hope, of life, of the future. It is a loss of warmth, and all things cherished. And there were never three lonelier people than Liz and John and Tommy Whittaker on that bitter cold December morning. They stood freezing at her graveside, among their friends, unable to tear themselves away from her, unable to bear leaving her there in the tiny white, flowered coffin.

"I can't," Liz said in a strangled voice to John after the service was over, and he knew immediately what she meant and clutched her arm, afraid she might slip into hysterics. They had been close to that for days, and Liz looked even worse now. "I can't leave her here . . . I can't . . ." She was choking on sobs, and in spite of her resistance, he pulled her closer.

"She's not here, Liz, she's gone . . . she's all right now."

"She's not all right. She's mine . . . I want her back . . . I want her back," she said, sobbing, as their friends drifted awkwardly away, not knowing how to help her. There was nothing one could do or say, nothing to ease the pain, or make it better. And Tommy stood there watching them, aching inside, pining for Annie.

"You all right, son?" his hockey coach asked him, as he drifted by, wiping tears from his cheeks without even trying to conceal them. Tommy started to nod yes, and then shook his head no, and collapsed into the burly man's arms, crying. "I know . . . I know . . . I lost my sister when I was twenty-one, and she was fifteen . . . it stinks . . . it really stinks. Just hang on to the memories . . . she was a cute little thing," he said, crying along with Tommy. "You hang on to all of it, son. She'll come back to you in little blessings all your life. Angels give us gifts like that . . . sometimes you don't even notice. But they're there. She's here. Talk to her some- times when you're alone . . . she'll hear you . . . you'll hear her . . . you'll never lose her." Tommy looked at him strangely for a minute, wondering if he was crazy, and then nodded. And his father had finally gotten his mother away from the grave by then, though barely. She could hardly walk by the time they got back to their car, and his father looked almost gray as he drove their car home, and none of them said a word to each other.

People dropped in all afternoon, and brought

them food. Some only left food or flowers on the front steps, afraid to bother them or face them. But there seemed to be a steady stream of people around constantly nonetheless, and there were others who stayed away, as though they felt that if they even touched the Whittakers, it could happen to them too. As though tragedy might be contagious.

Liz and John sat in the living room, looking exhausted and wooden, trying to welcome their friends, and relieved when it was late enough at night to lock their front door and stop answering the phone. And through it all, Tommy sat in his own room and saw no one. He walked past her room once or twice, but he couldn't bear it. Finally, he pulled the door closed so he wouldn't see it. All he could remember was how she had looked that last morning, so sick, so lifeless, so pale, only hours before she left them. It was hard to remember now what she had looked like when she was well, when she was teasing him or laughing. Suddenly, all he could see was her face in the hospital bed, those last minutes when she had said "thank you . . ." and then died. He was haunted by her words, her face, the reasons for her death. Why had she died? Why had it happened? Why couldn't it have been him instead of Annie? But he told no one what he felt, he said nothing to anyone. In fact, for the rest of the week, the Whittakers said nothing to each other. They just spoke to their friends when they had to, and in his case, he didn't.

New Year's Eve came and went like any other day in the year, and New Year's Day went unnoticed. Two days later he went back to school, and no one said anything to him. Everyone knew what had happened. His hockey coach was nice to him, but he never mentioned his own sister again, or Annie. No one said anything to Tommy about any of it, and he had nowhere to go with his grief. Suddenly, even Emily, the girl he had been flirting with awkwardly for months, seemed like an affront to him because he had discussed her with Annie. Everything reminded him of what he had lost, and he couldn't bear it. He hated the constant pain, like a severed limb, and the fact that he knew everyone looked at him with pity. Or maybe they thought he was strange. They didn't say anything to him. They left him alone, and that's how he stayed. And so did his parents. After the initial flurry of visitors, they stopped seeing their friends. They almost stopped seeing each other. Tommy never ate with them anymore. He couldn't bear sitting at their kitchen table without Annie, couldn't bring himself to go home in the afternoon and not share milk and cookies with her. He just couldn't stand being in his house without her. So he stayed at practice as long as he could, and then ate the dinner his mother left for him in the kitchen. Most of the time, he ate it standing up, next to the stove, and then dumped half of it into the garbage. The rest of the time he took a handful of cookies to his room with a glass of milk and skipped dinner completely. His mother never seemed to eat at all anymore, and his father seemed to come home later and later from work, and he was never hungry either. Real dinners seemed to be a thing of the past for all of them, time together something they all feared and avoided. It was as though they all knew that if the three of them were together, the absence of the fourth would be too unbearably painful. So they hid, each of them separately, from themselves, and from each other.

Everything reminded them of her, everything awoke their pain like a throbbing nerve that only quieted down for an occasional second, and the rest of the time, the pain it caused was almost beyond bearing.

His coach saw what was happening to him, and one of his teachers mentioned it just before spring vacation. For the first time in his entire school career, his grades had slipped and he seemed not to care about anything anymore. Not without Annie.

"The Whittaker boy's in a bad way," his homeroom teacher commented to the math teacher one day at the faculty table in the cafeteria. "I was going to call his mother last week, and then I saw her downtown. She looks worse than he does. I think they all took it pretty hard when their little girl died last winter."

"Who wouldn't?" the math teacher said sympathetically. She had kids of her own, and couldn't imagine how she'd survive it. "How bad is it? Is he flunking anything?"

"Not yet, but he's getting close," she said honestly. "He used to be one of my top students. I know how strongly his parents feel about education. His father even talked about sending him to an Ivy League college, if he wanted to go, and had the grades. He sure doesn't now."

"He can pull himself up again. It's only been three months. Give the kid a chance. I think we ought to leave them alone, him and his parents, and see how he does by the end of the school year. We can always call them if he really goes off the deep end and fails an exam or something."

"I just hate to see him slide down the tubes this way."

"Maybe he has no choice. Maybe right now he has to fight just to survive what happened. Maybe that's more important. Hard as it is for me to admit sometimes, there are more important things in life than social studies and trig. Let's give the kid a chance to catch his breath and regain his balance."

"It's been three months," the other teacher reminded. It was already late March by then. Eisenhower had been in the White House for two months, the Salk polio vaccine had tested successfully, and Lucille Ball had finally had her much publicized baby. The world was moving on rapidly, but not for Tommy Whittaker. His life had stopped with the death of Annie.

"Listen, it would take me a lifetime to get over

that, if it were my kid," the more sympathetic of the two teachers said softly.

"I know." The two teachers fell silent, thinking of their own families, and by the end of lunch agreed to let Tommy slide for a while longer. But everyone had noticed it. He seemed not to take an interest in anything. He had even decided not to play basketball or baseball that spring, although the coach was trying to convince him. And at home his room was a mess, his chores were never done, and for the first time in his life, he seemed to be constantly at odds with his parents.

But they were at odds with each other too. His mother and father seemed to argue constantly, and one of them was always loudly blaming the other for something. They hadn't put gas in the car, taken out the garbage, let out the dog, paid the bills, mailed the checks, bought coffee, answered a letter. It was all unimportant stuff, but all they ever did anymore was argue. His father was never home. His mother never smiled. And no one seemed to have a kind word for anyone. They didn't even seem sad anymore, just angry. They were furious, at each other, at the world, at life, at the fates that had so cruelly taken Annie from them. But no one ever said that. They just yelled and complained about everything else, like the high cost of their light bill.

It was easier for Tommy just to stay away from them. He hung around outside in the garden most of the time, sitting under the back steps and thinking, and he had started smoking cigarettes. He had even taken a couple of beers once or twice. And sometimes he just sat outside, under the back steps, out of the endless rain that had been pelting them all month, and drank beer and smoked Camels. It made him feel terribly grown up, and once he had even smiled, thinking that if Annie could have seen him, she'd have been outraged. But she couldn't, and his parents didn't care anymore, so it didn't matter what he did. And besides, he was sixteen years old now. A grown-up.

"I don't give a damn if you are sixteen, Maribeth Robertson," her father said, on a March night in Onawa, Iowa, some two hundred and fifty miles from where Tommy sat slowly getting drunk on beer under his parents' back steps, watching the storm flatten his mother's flowers. "You're not going out in that flimsy dress, wearing a whole beauty store of makeup. Go wash your face, and take that dress off."

"Daddy, it's the spring dance. And everyone wears makeup and prom dresses." The girl her older brother had taken out two years before, at her age, had looked a whole lot racier and her father had never objected. But that was Ryan's girlfriend, and that was different of course. Ryan could do anything. He was a boy, Maribeth wasn't.

"If you want to go out, you'll wear a decent

dress, or you can stay home and listen to the radio with your mother." The temptation to stay home was great, but then again, her sophomore prom would never come again. She was tempted not to go at all, especially not if she had to go in some dress that made her look like a nun, but she didn't really want to stay at home either. She had borrowed a dress from a friend's older sister, and it was a little bit too big, but she thought it was really pretty. It was a peacock blue taffeta, with dyed-to-match shoes that killed her feet because they were a size too small, but they were worth it. The dress was strapless, and had a little bolero jacket over it, but the low-cut strapless bodice showed off the cleavage that she'd been blessed with, and she knew that that was why her father had objected.

"Daddy, I'll keep the jacket on. I promise."

"Jacket or no jacket, you can wear that dress here at home with your mother. If you go to the dance, you'd best find something else to wear, or you can forget the dance. And frankly, I wouldn't mind if you did. All those girls look like sluts in those low-cut dresses. You don't need to show off your body to catch a boy's eye, Maribeth. You'd best learn that early on, or you'll be bringing home the worst sort of boy, mark my words," he said sternly, and her younger sister Noelle rolled her eyes. She was only thirteen and a great deal more rebellious than Maribeth had ever dreamed of being. Maribeth was a good girl, and so was Noelle, but she wanted more excitement out of life than Maribeth did. Even at thirteen, her eyes danced every time a boy whistled. At sixteen, Maribeth was a lot shyer, and a lot more cautious about defying their father.

In the end, Maribeth went to her room, and lay on her bed, crying, but her mother came in and helped her find something to wear. She didn't have much, but she had a nice navy blue dress with a white collar and long sleeves that Margaret Robertson knew her husband would deem suitable. But even seeing the dress brought tears to Maribeth's eyes. It was ugly.

"Mom, I'll look like a nun. Everyone will laugh me out of the gym." She looked heartbroken when she saw the dress her mother had chosen for her. It was a dress she had always hated.

"Not everyone will be wearing dresses like that, Maribeth," she said, pointing at the borrowed blue one. It was a pretty dress, she had to admit, but it frightened her a little bit too. It made Maribeth look like a woman. At sixteen, she had been blessed, or cursed, with full breasts, small hips, a tiny waist, and long lovely legs. Even in plain clothes, it was hard to conceal her beauty. She was taller than most of her friends, and she had developed very early.

It took an hour to talk her into wearing the dress, and by then her father had been sitting in the front room, grilling her date without subtlety or mercy. He was a boy Maribeth hardly knew and he looked extremely nervous as Mr.

47

Robertson questioned him about what kind of work he wanted to do when he finished school, and he admitted that he hadn't decided. Bert Robertson had explained to him by then that a little hard labor was good for a lad, and it wouldn't do him any harm either to go into the army. David O'Connor was agreeing frantically with him, with a look of growing desperation as Maribeth finally came reluctantly into the room, wearing the hated dress, and her mother's string of pearls to cheer it up a little. She had on flat navy shoes, instead of the peacock satin high heels she had hoped to wear, but she towered over David anyway, so she tried to tell herself it really didn't matter. She knew she looked terrible, and the dark dress was in somber contrast to the bright flame of her red hair, which made her even more self-conscious. She had never felt uglier, as she said hello to David.

"You look really nice," David said unconvincingly, wearing his older brother's dark suit, which was several sizes too big for him, as he handed her a corsage, but his hands were shaking too hard to pin it on, and her mother helped him.

"Have a good time," her mother said gently, feeling faintly sorry for her, as they left. In a way, she thought that she should have been allowed to wear the bright blue dress. It looked so pretty on her and she looked so grown up. But there was no point arguing with Bert once he made his mind up. And she knew how concerned he was about his daughters. Two of his sisters had been forced to get married years before, and he had always said to Margaret that he didn't care what it took, it wasn't going to happen to his daughters. They were going to be good girls, and marry nice boys. There were to be no tarts in his house, no illicit sex, no wild goings-on, and he had never made any bones about it. Only Ryan was allowed to do whatever he wanted. He was a boy, after all. He was eighteen now, and worked in Bert's business with him. Bert Robertson had the most successful car repair shop in Onawa, and at three dollars an hour, he ran a damn fine business, and was proud of it.

Ryan liked working for him, and claimed he was as good a mechanic as his father. They got on well, and sometimes on weekends, they went hunting and fishing together, and Margaret stayed home with the girls, and went to the movies with them, or caught up on her sewing. She had never worked, and Bert was proud of that too. He was by no means a rich man, but he could hold his head up all over town, and no daughter of his was going to change that by borrowing a dress and going to the spring dance dressed like an oversexed peacock. She was a pretty girl, but that was all the more reason to keep her down, and see that she didn't go wild like his sisters.

He had married a plain girl; Margaret O'Brien had wanted to become a nun before he met her.

And she had been a fine wife to him for nearly twenty years. But he'd never have married her if she'd looked like a fancy piece, the way Maribeth had just tried to do, or given him a lot of arguments, the way Noelle did. A son was a lot easier than a daughter, he'd concluded years before, though Maribeth had certainly never given him any trouble. But she had odd ideas, about women and what they could and couldn't do, about going to school, and even college. Her teachers had filled her head with ideas about how smart she was. And there was nothing wrong with a girl getting an education, to a point, as far as Bert was concerned, as long as she knew when to stop, and when to use it. Bert said frequently that you didn't need to go to college to learn to change a diaper. But a little schooling would have been fine to help him with his business, and he wouldn't mind if she studied bookkeeping and helped him with his books eventually, but some of her crazy ideas were right off the planet. Women doctors, female engineers, women lawyers, even nursing seemed like pushing it to Bert. What the hell was she talking about? Sometimes he really wondered. Girls were supposed to behave themselves so they didn't ruin their lives, or anyone else's, and then they were supposed to get married and have kids, as many as their husbands could afford or said they wanted. And then they were supposed to take care of their husbands and kids, and their home, and not give anyone a lot of trouble. He had told Ryan as much, he'd

50

warned him not to marry some wild girl, and not to get anyone pregnant he didn't want to have to marry. But the girls were another story entirely. They were supposed to behave . . . and not go out half naked to a dance, or drive their families crazy with half-cocked ideas about women. Sometimes he wondered if the movies Margaret took them to gave them crazy ideas. It certainly wasn't Margaret. She was a quiet woman who had never given him any trouble about anything. But Maribeth. She was another story completely. She was a good girl, but Bert had always thought that her modern ideas would cause a lot of trouble.

Maribeth and David reached the prom more than an hour late, and everyone seemed to be having a good time without them. Although they weren't supposed to drink at the dance, some of the boys in her class already looked drunk, and a few of the girls did too. And she had noticed several couples at the dance in parked cars as they arrived, but she had tried not to notice. It was embarrassing seeing that with David. She hardly knew him, and they weren't really friends, but no one else had asked her to the dance, and she'd wanted to go, just so she could see it, and be there, and see what it was like. She was tired of being left out of everything. She never fit in. She was always different. For years, she had been at the top of her class, and some of the other kids hated her for it, the rest of them just ignored her.

And her parents always embarrassed her whenever they came to school. Her mother was such a mouse, and her father was loud and told everyone what to do, especially her mother. She had never stood up to him. She was cowed by him, and agreed with everything he said, even when he was so obviously wrong. And he was so outspoken about all of his opinions, of which he had several million, mostly about women, their role in life, the importance of men, and the unimportance of education. He always held himself up as an example. He had been an orphan from Buffalo, and had made good in spite of a sixth-grade education. According to him, no one needed more than that, and the fact that her brother had bothered to finish high school had been nothing short of a miracle. He had been a terrible student, and had been suspended constantly for his behavior, but as long as it was Ryan and not the girls, her father thought it was amusing. Ryan would have probably been a Marine by then, and gone to Korea, if he hadn't been 4-F because of flat feet and the knee he had wrecked playing football. She and Ryan had very little to say to each other. It was always hard for her to imagine that they came from the same family, and had been born on the same planet.

He was good-looking and arrogant, and not very bright, and it was hard to imagine they were even related. "What *do* you care about?" she asked him one day, trying to figure out who he was, and maybe who she was in relation to him, and he looked at her in amazement, wondering why she had even asked him.

"Cars, girls . . . beer . . . having a good time . . . Dad talks about work all the time. It's okay, I guess . . . as long as I get to work on cars, and don't have to work in a bank or an insurance company or something. I guess I'm pretty lucky to work for Dad."

"I guess," she said softly, nodding, looking at him with her big, questioning green eyes, and trying to respect him. "Do you ever want to be more than that?"

"Like what?" He seemed puzzled by the question.

"Like anything. More than just working for Dad. Like going to Chicago, or New York, or having a better job . . . or going to college . . ." Those were her dreams. She wanted so much more, and she had no one to share her dreams with. Even the girls in her class were different than she was. No one could ever figure out why she cared about grades or studies. What difference did it make? Who cared? She did. But as a result, she had no friends, and had to go to the dance with boys like David.

But she still had her dreams. No one could take those from her. Not even her father. Maribeth wanted a career, a more interesting place to live, an exciting job, an education if she could ever afford one, and eventually a husband she loved and respected. She couldn't imagine a life with someone she didn't admire. She couldn't imagine a life like her mother's, married to a man who paid no attention to her at all, never listened to her ideas, and didn't care what she was thinking. She wanted so much more. She had so many dreams, so many ideas that everyone thought were crazy, except her teachers, who knew how exceptional she was, and wanted to help her be free of the bonds that held her. They knew how important it would be for her one day to get an education. But the only time she ever got to let her soul out a little bit was when she wrote papers for one of her classes, and then she would be praised for her ideas . . . but only then, for one fleeting moment. She never got to talk to anyone about them.

"Do you want some punch?" David asked her.

"Huh? . . ." Her mind had been a million miles away. "I'm sorry . . . I was thinking about something else . . . I'm sorry my father chewed your ear off tonight. We got in a fight about my dress, and I had to change." She felt more awkward than ever as she said it.

"It's very nice," he said nervously, obviously lying. It was anything but, and she knew it. The navy dress was so tired and plain, it had taken a lot of courage to wear it. But she was used to being different and ridiculed. Or she should have been. She was always the odd man out, always had been. It was why David O'Connor had felt comfortable asking her to the dance. He knew no one else would. She was good-looking, but she was weird, everyone said so. She was too tall, she had bright red hair, and a great figure, but all she cared about was school, and she never went on dates. No one asked her. He figured she'd say yes to him and he was right. He didn't play sports, and he was short, and he had terrible problems with his complexion. Who else could he have asked, except Maribeth Robertson? She'd been the only choice except for some really ugly girls he wouldn't have wanted to be caught dead with. And actually, he liked Maribeth. He just wasn't so crazy about her father. The old man had really made him sweat it while he waited for her. He'd been wondering if he was going to be stuck there all night, when she finally appeared in the dark blue dress with the white collar. And she looked okay. You could still see her great figure, even under the ugly dress. What difference did it make anyway? He was excited about dancing with her, and feeling her body next to his. Just thinking about it gave him a hard-on.

"Do you want some punch?" he asked her again, and she nodded. She didn't, but she didn't know what else to say to him. She was sorry she had come now. He was such a drip, and no one else was going to ask her to dance, and she looked dumb in the dark blue dress. She should have stayed home and listened to the radio with her mother, just as her father had threatened. "I'll be right back," David reassured her, and disap-

55

peared, as she watched the other couples dancing. Most of the girls looked beautiful to her, and their dresses were brightly colored and had big skirts and little jackets, like the one she'd almost worn but hadn't been allowed to.

It seemed like ages before David appeared again, and when he did, he was smiling. He looked as though he had an exciting secret, and as soon as she tasted the punch, she knew why he looked so happy. It had a funny taste to it, and she figured that someone had spiked it.

"What's in this?" she asked, taking a big sniff and a small sip to confirm her suspicions. She had only tasted alcohol a few times, but she was pretty sure the punch had been doctored.

"Just a little happy juice," he grinned, looking suddenly shorter and a whole lot worse than he had when he'd asked her. He was a real jerk and the way he leered at her was disgusting.

"I don't want to get drunk," she said matter-of-factly, sorry that she had come, especially with him. As usual, she felt like a fish out of water.

"Come on, Maribeth, be a sport. You won't get drunk. Just have a few sips. It'll make you feel good."

She looked at him more closely then, and realized that he'd been drinking while he went to get their drinks. "How many have you had?"

"The juniors have a couple of bottles of rum out behind the gym, and Cunningham has a pint of vodka."

"Great. How terrific."

"Yeah, isn't it?" He smiled happily, glad she didn't object, and totally oblivious to her tone. She was looking down at him in disgust, but he didn't seem to notice.

"I'll be back," she said coolly, seeming years older than he was. Her height and her demeanor made her seem older than she was most of the time, and next to him she looked like a giant, though she was only five feet eight, but David was a good four or five inches shorter.

"Where are you going?" He looked worried. They hadn't danced yet.

"The ladies' room," she said coolly.

"I hear they have a pint in there too."

"I'll bring you some," she said, and disappeared into the crowd. The band was playing "In the Cool, Cool, Cool of the Evening," and the kids were dancing cheek to cheek, and all she felt was sad as she made her way out of the gym, past a group of guys obviously trying to hide a bottle. But they couldn't hide the effects of it, and a few feet further on, two of them were throwing up against the wall. But she was used to that from her brother. She walked as far away as she could, and went to sit on a bench on the other side of the gym, just to gather her wits and pass a little time before she went back to David. He was obviously going to get drunk and she was not having fun. She should probably just walk home and forget the whole thing. She doubted if after a few drinks David would even notice her absence.

She sat on the bench for a long time, getting chilled in the night air, and not really caring. It felt good just to be there, away from all of them, David, the kids in her class, and the ones she didn't know, the ones drinking and throwing up. It felt good to be away from her parents too. For a minute she wished that she could sit there forever. She laid her head back against the bench and closed her eyes, and stretched her legs out ahead of her, as she just floated in the cool air, thinking.

"Too much to drink?" a voice asked softly next to her, and she jumped as she heard it. She looked up to see a familiar face. He was a senior, and a football star, and he had no idea who she was. She couldn't imagine what he was doing there, or why he bothered to talk to her. Maybe he thought she was someone else. She sat up and shook her head, expecting him to walk off and leave her.

"No. Just too many people. Too much everything, I guess."

"Yeah, me too," he said, sitting down next to her, uninvited, and it was impossible not to notice how handsome he was, even in the moonlight. "I hate crowds."

"That's a little hard to believe," she said, sounding amused, and feeling oddly comfortable with him, even though he was a hero on campus. But it was all so unreal here, sitting outside the gym, on a bench in the dark. "You're always surrounded by people."

"And you? How do you know who I am?" He sounded intrigued, and looked gorgeous. "Who are you?"

"I'm Cinderella. My Buick just turned into a pumpkin, and my date turned into a drunk, and I came out here looking for my glass slipper. Have you seen it?"

"Possibly. Describe it. How do I know you're really Cinderella?" He was amused by her, and he wondered why he had never noticed her before. She was wearing an ugly dress, but she had a great face, and figure, and a good sense of humor. "Are you a senior?" He looked interested suddenly, although everyone in school knew he'd been going with Debbie Flowers ever since they were sophomores. There was even a rumor that they were going to get married after graduation.

"I'm a sophomore," she said with a wry smile, surprisingly honest, even when confronted by Prince Charming.

"Maybe that's why I never noticed," he said honestly. "But you look older."

"Thanks, I guess." She smiled at him, thinking that she should either go back to David, or start walking home. She shouldn't be sitting there all alone with a senior. But she felt safe here.

"My name's Paul Browne. What's yours, Cinderella?"

"Maribeth Robertson." She smiled and stood up.

"Where are you going?" He was tall, with dark hair and a dazzling smile, and he looked disappointed.

"I was just going home."

"Alone?" She nodded. "Want a lift?"

"I'm fine, thanks." She couldn't believe she was turning down a ride with Paul Browne, star senior. Who would have believed it? She grinned, thinking about it, what an achievement.

"Come on, I'll walk you back to the gym at least. Are you going to tell your date you're leaving?"

"I should, I guess." They walked easily back to the main entrance of the gym, like old friends, and as soon as they approached, she saw David, already hopelessly drunk, sharing a bottle unsteadily with half a dozen friends. There were monitors inside, but in spite of them, the kids seemed to be doing what they wanted. "I don't think I need to tell him anything," Maribeth said discreetly, and stopped long before they reached him, looking up at Paul with a smile. He was a lot taller than she was. "Thanks for keeping me company. I'm going to go home now." The evening had been a total waste for her. She'd had a rotten time, except for talking to Paul Browne.

"I can't let you go home alone. Come on, let me give you a ride, or are you afraid my Chevy will turn into a pumpkin too?"

"I don't think so. Aren't you the handsome prince?" she asked, teasing him, but then feeling embarrassed. He really was the handsome prince, and she knew she shouldn't have said it.

"Am I?" he quipped, looking incredibly handsome and sophisticated as he helped her into his car. It *was* an impeccably kept 1951 Bel Air with the new chrome trim, and the inside was all red leather.

"I like your pumpkin, Paul," she teased, and he laughed, and when she gave him her address, he suggested they go out for a hamburger and a milkshake.

"You can't have had much fun. Your date looked like a creep . . . sorry, maybe I shouldn't have said that . . . but he certainly didn't do much for you tonight. I'll bet you didn't even get a dance. You might as well go out for a little fun on the way home. What do you think? It's early." It was and she didn't have to be home till midnight.

"Okay," she said cautiously, wanting to be with him, and more impressed with him than she wanted to admit. It was impossible not to be. "Did you come alone tonight?" she asked, wondering what had happened to Debbie.

"Yes, I did. I'm a free agent again." He suspected from the way Maribeth had asked that she knew about Debbie. Everyone at school did. But they had broken up two days before, because Debbie had found out that he'd gone out with someone else over Christmas vacation, but he didn't explain that. "I guess that was lucky for me, huh Maribeth?" He smiled disarmingly, and asked her questions about herself, as they drove to Willie's, the diner where all the popular kids hung out at all hours of the day and night. And when they got there, the jukebox was blaring and the place was jammed. It looked like more kids than at the dance, and suddenly she was more conscious than ever of the ugly dress her parents had made her wear, and of who he was. Suddenly she felt every minute of sixteen, and less. And Paul was nearly eighteen. But it was as though he sensed her shyness, as he introduced her to all his friends. Some of them raised their eyebrows questioningly, wanting to know who she was, but no one seemed to object to her joining them. They were surprisingly nice to her, as Paul's guest, and she had a good time, laughing and talking. She shared a cheeseburger with him, and a milkshake, and they danced to half a dozen songs on the jukebox, including a couple of slow dances, when he held her breathtakingly close to him, and felt her breasts pressed against him. And she could instantly feel the effect on him, which embarrassed her, but he wouldn't let her pull away, and he held her close to him as they danced, and then looked down and smiled at her gently.

"Where have you been for the last four years, little girl?" he said, sounding hoarse, and she smiled in answer.

"I think you've been too busy to notice where I've been," she said honestly, and he liked that about her.

"I think you're right, and I've been a fool.

This must be my lucky night." He pulled her closer again and let his lips drift against her hair. There was something about her that excited him. It wasn't just her body, or the spectacular breasts he'd encountered while they were dancing, it was something about the way she looked at him, the way she responded to him. There was something very bright and brash and brave about her, as though she weren't afraid of anything. He knew she was only a kid, and a sophomore would have to be a little intimidated by a senior, and yet she wasn't. She wasn't afraid of him, or of saying what she thought, and he liked that about her. Breaking up with Debbie had bruised his ego, and Maribeth was just the balm he needed to soothe it.

They got back in his car, and he turned to look at her. He didn't want to take her home. He liked being with her. He liked everything about her. And for her, it was a heady experience just being with him.

"Do you want to go for a little drive? It's only eleven." They had left the dance so early, they'd had plenty of time to talk and dance at Willie's.

"I should probably get home," she said cautiously, as he started the car, but he headed in the direction of the park, instead of her house. It didn't worry her, but she didn't want to stay out too late. She felt safe with him though. He had been a perfect gentleman all night, a lot more so than David.

"Just a little spin, then I'll take you home, I

promise. I just don't want the night to end. This has been special for me," he said meaningfully, and she could feel her head reeling with excitement. Paul Browne? What if this was for real? What if he went steady with her instead of Debbie Flowers? She couldn't believe it. "I've had a great time, Maribeth."

"Me too. A lot better than I had at the dance," she laughed. They chatted easily for a few minutes after that, until he drove into a secluded area near a lake, stopped the car, and turned to face her.

"You're a special girl," he said, and there was no doubt in Maribeth's mind that he meant it. He opened the glove compartment then and pulled out a pint bottle of gin and offered it to her. "Would you like a little drink?"

"No, thanks. I don't drink."

"How come?" He seemed surprised.

"I don't really like it." He thought that was odd, but he offered it to her anyway. She started to decline, but as he insisted, she took a little sip, not to hurt his feelings. The clear liquid burned her throat and her eyes as it went down, and there was a hot feeling in her mouth afterwards, and she felt flushed, as he leaned over and pulled her into his arms and kissed her.

"Do you like that better than gin?" he asked sensuously after he'd kissed her again, and she smiled and nodded, feeling worldly and excited and a little sinful. He was so incredibly exciting, and so unbelievably handsome. "So do I," he

said, and kissed her again, and this time, he unbuttoned the prim dress as she tried to keep the
buttons done up, but his fingers were nimbler
than hers and more practiced, and within sec-
onds, he was holding her breasts and fondling
them as he kissed her breathlessly and she had
no idea how to stop him.

"Paul, don't . . . please . . ." she said softly,
wanting to mean it, but she didn't. She knew
what she had to do, but it was so hard not to
want him. He leaned down then and kissed her
breasts, and suddenly her bra was undone, and
the top of her dress was completely open. His
mouth was on her breasts, and then her lips and
then he was working her nipples with his fingers.
And she moaned in spite of herself as he slid a
hand under her skirt, and found her expertly and
quickly, despite her attempt to keep her legs together. But she had to keep reminding herself
that she didn't want what he was doing to her.
She wanted it to frighten her, and yet nothing
he did scared her. Everything he did was exciting
and delicious, but she knew she had to stop, and
finally she pulled away, out of breath and out
of control, and she looked at him with regret
and shook her head, and he understood it.

"I can't. I'm sorry, Paul." She was stunned
by all he had made her feel. Her head was spin-
ning.

"It's all right," he said gently, "I know . . . I
shouldn't have . . . I'm really sorry . . ." And
as he said the words, he kissed her again and

they started all over again, and this time it was even harder to stop, and they both looked completely disheveled, as she pulled away from him, and she saw in shock that his fly was open. He pulled her hand toward him then, and she tried to will herself not to, but she was fascinated by what he was doing. This was what she had been warned about, what she had been told never to do, yet it was all so overwhelming, she couldn't stop herself, or him, and he leapt into her hands as he pressed her hand into his zipper, and she found herself caressing him, and stroking him, as he kissed her and laid her down on the seat, and lay on top of her, pulsating with desire and excitement. "Oh God . . . Maribeth, I want you so much . . . oh baby . . . I love you . . ." He pushed her skirt up then, and his own trousers down, with what seemed like a single movement, and she felt him pressing against her, searching for her, needing her desperately, as she now needed him, and with a single surge of pleasure and pain, he entered her, and barely moving inside of her, he gave a huge shudder beyond his control, and came less than a moment later. "Oh God . . . oh God . . . oh Maribeth . . ." And then as he returned slowly to earth, he looked at her, as she stared at him in shock, unable to believe what they'd done, and he gently touched her face with his fingers. "Oh God, Maribeth, I'm sorry . . . you were a virgin . . . I couldn't help myself . . . you're so beautiful and I wanted you so badly . . . I'm sorry, baby . . ."

"It's all right," she found herself reassuring him, as he lay still within her, and slowly withdrew, already getting excited again, but he didn't dare try for another. And he pulled a towel miraculously from under the seat, and tried to help her make repairs, while she tried desperately not to be embarrassed. He took a long swig of gin then, and then offered it to her, and this time she took it, wondering if the first sip had made her succumb to his advances, or if she was in love with him, or he with her, or what it all meant, and if she was his steady girl now.

"You're incredible," he said, kissing her again, and pulling her close to him on the seat. "I'm sorry it happened here, like this tonight. Next time will be better, I promise. My parents are going out of town in two weeks, you can come to my place." It never occurred to him for a single moment that she might not want to continue to do that with him. He assumed she wanted more, and he wasn't entirely wrong, but for the most part, Maribeth wasn't sure what she was feeling. Her whole world had turned upside down in a matter of minutes.

"Did you . . . and . . . Debbie . . ." She knew even before the words were out that it was a stupid question, and he smiled at her, looking for a moment like a much wiser older brother.

"You are young, aren't you? Come to think of it, how old are you?"

"I turned sixteen two weeks ago."

"Well, you're a big girl now." He took off his

jacket and put it around her shoulders when he saw she was shaking. She was in shock over what they'd done, and then she knew she had to ask him a question.

"Could I get pregnant from that?" The very thought terrified her, but he looked reassuring. And she really wasn't sure how great a risk she might have taken.

"I don't think so. Not from one time like that. I mean you could . . . but you won't, Maribeth. And next time I'll be careful." She wasn't quite sure what being careful entailed, but she knew that if she ever did it again, and she might, maybe if they went steady, if Debbie Flowers had and that was what he expected of her, then she knew she would want to be careful. The one thing she didn't want in her life now was a baby. Even the remotest possibility of it made her tremble. And she didn't want to be forced into marriage, like her two aunts. She suddenly remembered all of her father's stories.

"How will I know if I am?" she asked him honestly, as he started the engine, and he turned to look at her, surprised by how innocent she was. She had seemed so grown up to him earlier in the evening.

"Don't you know?" he asked, more than a little stunned, and she shook her head, as always honest. "You'll miss your period." She was embarrassed to hear him say it, and she nodded her understanding. But she still really didn't know any more about it. She didn't want to question him any further now, or he might think she was incredibly stupid.

He said very little as he drove her home, and he seemed to look around as they stopped in front of her house, and then he turned to her and kissed her. "Thanks, Maribeth. I had a wonderful evening." Somehow she expected losing her virginity to mean more than just a "wonderful evening," and yet she had no right to expect more of him, and she knew it. She had been wrong to do it with him the first night she met him, and she knew she'd be lucky if it developed into something more. And yet he had told her he loved her.

"I had a wonderful evening too," she said cautiously and politely. "See you at school," she said, sounding hopeful. She handed his jacket back to him, and she hurried from the car to her front steps. The door was open and she let herself in. It was two minutes before midnight. And she was grateful that everyone had already gone to bed. She didn't have to explain anything, or answer any questions. She cleaned herself as best she could, grateful that no one else was there to notice, and she soaked the skirt of her dress in water and then hung it up, trying not to cry. She could always say that someone had spilled punch on her, or gotten sick.

She slipped into her nightgown, shaking from head to foot, and hurried into bed, feeling sick, and then lay there in the dark, in the same room as Noelle, thinking of everything that had happened. Maybe this was the beginning of an important relationship in her life, she tried to reassure herself. But she wasn't sure what it all meant, or how serious Paul Browne was about her. She was thoughtful enough to wonder if he had meant everything he'd said. She hoped he had, but she'd heard other stories of girls who had gone all the way, and then been dumped by the guys who made them do it. But Paul hadn't "made her" do anything. That was the scary part. She had wanted to do it with him. That was the most shocking thing about it. She had wanted to make love to him. Once he had started touching her, she wanted him. And she wasn't even sorry now. She was just scared about what would happen. She lay in bed, terrified, for hours, praying she wouldn't get pregnant.

Her mother asked her if she'd had a good time the next morning over breakfast, and she said she had. The funny thing was that no one seemed to suspect anything, and from the way she felt, Maribeth expected them all to see that she was suddenly a different person. She was grown up, a woman now, she had done it, and she was in love with the most wonderful senior in the whole school. It was absolutely incredible to her that no one noticed.

Ryan was in a bad mood, Noelle had a fight with her mother about something she'd done the night before. Her father had gone to the shop, even though it was Saturday, and her mother said she had a headache. They all had their own lives, and no one saw that Maribeth had been transformed from caterpillar to butterfly, and had been Cinderella to Prince Charming.

She seemed to float on air all weekend, but on Monday she came to ground with a sharp thump, when she saw Paul walking into school with an arm around Debbie Flowers. And by noon everyone knew the tale. He and Debbie had had a fight, and had made up, because someone said he had gone out with some other girl over the weekend, and Debbie couldn't take it. No one knew who she was, but they seemed to know that Debbie had been furious, and by Sunday they had patched things up and were once again going steady. Maribeth felt her heart crash to the floor, and didn't see him face-to-face until Wednesday. He was very kind to her, and stopped to say something to her, as she tried to avert her face from him while she put something in her locker. She hoped he would walk by, but he had been looking for her for days and was glad he'd found her.

"Can we go and talk somewhere?" he asked in a low voice that seemed filled with sex appeal and raw emotion.

"I can't . . . I'm sorry . . . I'm late for P.E. Maybe later."

"Don't give me that." He grabbed her arm gently. "Look, I'm sorry about what happened . . . I meant it . . . I really did . . . I wouldn't have done that unless I thought . . . I'm sorry

. . . she's crazy, but we've been together for a long time. I didn't want you to get hurt." She almost cried when she saw that he really meant it. Why did he have to be a nice guy? But it would have been even worse if he hadn't.

"Don't worry about it. I'm fine."

"No, you're not," he said unhappily, feeling guiltier than ever about her.

"Yes, I am," she said, and then suddenly tears stung her eyes and she wished that everything could have been different. "Look, forget it."

"Just remember, I'm around if you need me." She wondered why he had said that, and she spent the next month trying to forget him. She ran into him everywhere, in the halls, outside the gym. Suddenly it seemed as though she couldn't avoid him. And in early May, six weeks after Maribeth and Paul made love, he and Debbie announced that they were engaged and getting married in July, after graduation. And on the same day, Maribeth discovered that she was pregnant.

She was only two weeks late, but she was throwing up constantly, and her whole body felt different. Her breasts seemed suddenly huge and were excruciatingly tender, her waist seemed to expand overnight, and at every moment of the day, she was overwhelmingly nauseous. She could hardly believe that her body could change so much so quickly. But every morning as she lay on the bathroom floor after throwing up, praying that no one had overheard her, she knew that she couldn't hide it forever.

She didn't know what to do, or who to tell, or where to turn, and she didn't want to tell Paul. But finally at the end of May, she went to her mother's doctor and begged him not to tell her parents. She cried so much that he agreed, reluctantly, and confirmed that she was pregnant. She was, predictably, exactly two months pregnant. And Paul had been wrong, she very emphatically could get pregnant from "just one time." She wondered if he'd been intentionally lying to her, or simply stupid, when he told her he didn't think it could happen. Maybe both. It was certainly beginner's luck, in any case, and she sat on the examining table, clutching the drape, with tears rolling down her cheeks, as the doctor asked her what she was going to do about it.

"Do you know who the baby's father is?" he asked, and Maribeth looked shocked and even more mortified at the question.

"Of course," she said, looking humiliated and grief-stricken. There was no easy way out of this dilemma.

"Will he marry you?" She shook her head, her red hair looking like flame, her eyes like green oceans. The full impact of it hadn't even hit her yet, though the prospect of forcing Paul to marry her, even if she could, was very tempting.

"He's engaged to someone else," she said hoarsely, and the doctor nodded.

"He might change his plans, under the circumstances. Men do that." He smiled sadly. He was sorry for her. She was a sweet girl, and it was inevitable that this would change her life forever.

"He won't change his plans," Maribeth said softly. She was the classic one-night stand, a girl he didn't even know, though he had told her he'd be around if she needed him. Well, she did now. But that didn't mean he would marry her just because he had gotten her pregnant.

"What are you going to tell your parents, Maribeth?" he asked soberly, and she closed her eyes, overwhelmed with the terror of it, just thinking about telling her father.

"I don't know yet."

"Would you like me to talk to them with you?" It was a kind offer, but she couldn't imagine letting him tell them for her. She knew that sooner or later she would have to do it.

"What about . . . about getting rid of it?" she asked bravely. She wasn't even completely sure how one did that, except that she knew that some women "got rid" of babies. She'd heard her mother and aunt discussing it once, and the word they had whispered was "abortion." Her mother had said that the woman almost died, but Maribeth knew that would be better than facing her father.

But the doctor frowned at her immediately. "That's costly, dangerous, and illegal. And I don't want to hear another word from you about it, young lady. At your age, the simplest solution is to have the baby and give it up for adoption. That's what most girls your age do. The baby is due in December. You could go to the Sisters of Charity the moment it showed, and stay there until you have the baby."

"You mean give it away?" He made it sound so simple, and somehow she suspected that it was more complicated than that, that there was more he wasn't saying about the process.

"That's right," he said, feeling sorry for her. She was so young, and so naive. But she had the body of a full-blown woman, and it had gotten her into trouble. "You wouldn't have to go into hiding for a while. It probably won't start to show until July or August, maybe even later than that. But you need to tell your parents." Maribeth nodded, feeling numb, but what could she tell them? That she'd made love to a boy she didn't know on the front seat of his car the night of the prom, and he wouldn't marry her? Maybe her mother would even want to keep the baby. She couldn't imagine any of it, or saying it to them, as she put her clothes back on and left his office. He had promised not to say anything to them, until she did, and she believed him.

She sought Paul out at school that afternoon. Graduation was in two weeks, and she knew it was wrong to put any pressure on him. It was as much her fault as his, or so she thought, but she couldn't forget what he'd told her.

She let him walk her slowly around the

grounds of school, and they wound up on the bench behind the gym, where they had first met the night of the dance and then she told him.

"Oh shit. You're not." He let out a long, slow sigh, and looked desperately unhappy.

"I am. I'm sorry, Paul. I don't even know why I told you. I just thought you should know." He nodded, unable to say much of anything for the moment.

"I'm getting married in six weeks. Debbie would kill me if she knew. I told her everything she heard about you were lies and rumors."

"What did she hear?" Maribeth looked curious, intrigued that Debbie had heard anything about her.

"That I went out with you that night. Everyone we saw at Willie's told her. We had broken up. It was reasonable. I just told her it was no big deal, and it didn't mean anything." But it hurt anyway to hear him say it. Debbie was the one who mattered to him. She wasn't.

"And did it mean anything?" Maribeth asked pointedly. She wanted to know. She had a right to know now. She was having his baby.

He looked at her thoughtfully for a time, and then nodded. "It meant something then. Maybe not as much as it should have, but it did. I thought you were terrific. But then Debbie hounded me all weekend, and she cried. She said I was treating her like dirt and cheating on her, and I owed her more than that after three years, so I said I'd marry her after graduation."

"Is that what you want?" Maribeth asked, staring at him, wondering who he was, and what he really wanted. She didn't really think Debbie was it for him, and wondered if he knew that.

"I don't know what I want. But I do know I don't want a baby."

"Neither do I." She was sure of it. She wasn't sure she'd ever want one, but surely not now, and not with him. No matter how handsome he was, it was obvious to her as they sat there that he didn't love her. She didn't want to be forced into marriage with him, even if he agreed to it, which she was sure he wouldn't. But she didn't want a man who would lie about her, or pretend he had never gone out with her, or cared about her. She wanted someone, eventually, who would be proud to love her, and have her baby. Not somebody who had to be railroaded into a shotgun wedding.

"Why don't you get rid of it?" he asked softly, and Maribeth looked at him sadly.

"You mean, give it away?" That was what she was planning to do, and what the doctor had suggested.

"No. I mean have an abortion. I know a senior who did last year. I could ask around. Maybe I could scrounge up some money. It's really expensive."

"No, I don't want to, Paul." The doctor had discouraged her from exploring that avenue any further. And she was uncomfortable too, no matter how little she knew, that getting rid of it might be murder.

"Are you going to keep it?" he asked, sounding panicked. What was Debbie going to say? She'd kill him.

"No. I'm going to give it away," she said. She had thought about it a lot. And it seemed like the only solution. "The doctor says I can live with the nuns once it shows, and then give it to them, and they'll put it up for adoption." And then she turned, and asked him a strange question. "Would you want to see it?" But he shook his head, and then turned away. He hated how she made him feel, inadequate and frightened, and angry. He knew that he was being less than he should to her. But he didn't have the guts to take this on with her. And he didn't want to lose Debbie.

"I'm sorry, Maribeth. I feel like such an S.O.B." She wanted to tell him that he was, but she couldn't. She wanted to say she understood, but she couldn't do that either, because she didn't. She didn't understand anything. What had happened to them, why they had done it, why she had gotten pregnant, and why he was going to be marrying Debbie instead of her, while she hid with the nuns and had his baby. It was all so out of control.

They sat in silence for a little while after that, and then he left, and she knew she'd never speak to him again. She only saw him once, the day before graduation, and he didn't say anything to her. He just looked at her, and then turned away, and she walked back across the campus alone, with tears streaming down her face, not wanting to have his baby. It was all so unfair, and she was feeling sicker every day.

The week after school let out, she was kneeling over the toilet one day, puking her brains out, and she had forgotten to lock the door, when her brother came in and saw her.

"Sorry, Sis . . . oh my God . . . are you sick?" Ryan looked instantly sorry for her, and then just as quickly a light dawned, and he stared as she vomited again and he understood. "Shit, you're pregnant." It was a statement, not a question.

She lay there, with her head resting on the toilet for a long time, and then finally she stood up, and he was still staring at her, his face devoid of sympathy, only filled with accusation. "Dad's going to kill you."

"What makes you so sure I'm pregnant?" She tried to sound flip with him, but he knew her better.

"Who's the guy?"

"None of your business," she said, feeling a wave of nausea sweep over her again, more out of nerves and terror.

"You'd better tell him to get out his good suit, or start running. Dad'll have his ass if he doesn't do right by you."

"Thanks for the advice," she said, and walked slowly out of the bathroom. But she knew now that her days were numbered. And she was right.

79

Ryan told her father that afternoon, and he came home in a rage and nearly tore off the door to her bedroom. She was lying there on the bed, while Noelle listened to records and did her nails. And he pulled Maribeth into the living room and shouted for her mother. Maribeth had been trying to think about how she was going to tell them, but now she didn't have to. Ryan had done it for her.

Her mother was already crying by the time she came out of her room, and Ryan looked grim, as though she had wronged him too. Her father had told Noelle to stay in their room. And he was like a raging bull as he stormed around the living room, telling Maribeth how she was just like her aunts, and had behaved like a whore, and dishonored them all. And then he demanded to know who had gotten her pregnant. But she was prepared for that. She didn't care what they did to her. She wasn't going to tell them.

She had thought Paul was dazzling and exciting, and she would have loved to fall in love with him, and have him want her. But he wasn't in love with her, and he was marrying someone else. She didn't want to start her life out like that, at sixteen, and ruin it completely. She'd rather have the baby, and give it away. And they couldn't force her to tell them.

"Who is he?" her father shouted at her again and again. "I'm not letting you out of this room until you tell me."

"Then we'll be here for a long time," she said quietly. She had done so much thinking since she'd found out that even her father didn't scare her. Besides, the worst had happened now. She was pregnant. They knew. What more could they do to her?

"Why won't you tell us who he is? Is it a teacher? A kid? A married man? A priest? One of your brother's friends? Who is it?"

"It doesn't matter. He's not going to marry me," she said calmly, surprised at her own strength in the eye of the hurricane that was her father.

"Why not?" he raged on.

"Because he doesn't love me, and I don't love him. It's as simple as that."

"It doesn't sound simple to me," her father said, sounding even angrier, while her mother cried and wrung her hands. Maribeth felt terrible as she looked at her. She hated hurting her mother. "It sounds like you were sleeping with some guy, and didn't even love him. That's about as rotten as you get. Even your aunts loved the men they slept with. They married them. They had decent lives, and legitimate children. And what are you going to do with this baby?"

"I don't know, Dad. I thought I'd put it up for adoption, unless . . ."

"Unless what? You think you're going to keep it here, and disgrace yourself and us? Over my dead body, and your mother's." Her mother

81

looked imploringly at her, begging her to undo this disaster, but there was no way for her to do that.

"I don't want to keep the baby, Dad," she said sadly, as tears came to her eyes at last. "I'm sixteen, I can't give it anything, and I want a life too. I don't want to give up my life because I can't do anything for it. We both have a right to more than that."

"How noble of you," he said, furious with her beyond words. "It would have been nice if you could have been a little more noble before you took your pants off. Look at your brother, he plays around with lots of girls. He's never gotten anyone pregnant. Look at you, sixteen and your damn life is down the toilet."

"It doesn't have to be that way, Dad. I can go to school with the nuns while I stay with them, and then go back to school in December, after I have the baby. I could go back after Christmas vacation. We could say I've been sick."

"Really? And just who do you think would believe that? You think people won't talk? Everyone will know. You'll be a disgrace, and so will we. You'll be a disgrace to this whole family."

"Then what do you want me to do, Dad?" she asked miserably, tears streaming down her face now. This was even harder than she'd thought it would be, and there were no easy solutions. "What do you want me to do? Die? I can't undo what I did. I don't know what to do. There's no way to make this better." She was sobbing, but he looked unmoved. He looked icy.

"You'll just have to have the baby and put it up for adoption."

"Do you want me to stay with the nuns?" she asked, hoping he would tell her she could stay at home. Living at the convent away from her family terrified her. But if he told her to leave, she had nowhere else to go.

"You can't stay here," her father said firmly, "and you can't keep the baby. Go to the Sisters of Charity, give up the baby, and then come home." And then he dealt the final blow to her soul. "I don't want to see you until then. And I don't want you seeing your mother or your sister." For a moment she thought his words would kill her. "What you've done is an insult to us, and to yourself. You've hurt your dignity, and ours. You've broken our trust. You've disgraced us, Maribeth, and yourself. Don't ever forget that."

"Why is what I did so terrible? I never lied to you. I never hurt you. I never betrayed you. I was very stupid. Once. And look what's happening to me for it. Isn't this enough? I can't get out of it. I'm going to have to live with it. I'm going to have to give up my baby. Isn't that enough for you? Just how much do I have to be punished?" She was sobbing and heartbroken, but he was relentless.

"That's between you and God. I'm not punishing you. He is."

"You're my father. You're sending me away from here. You're telling me that you won't see me again until I give away the baby . . . you're forbidding me to see my sister and my mother." And she knew her mother would never disobey him. She knew how weak her mother was, how unable to make her own decisions, how swayed she was by him. They were all closing the door on her, and Paul already had. She was totally alone now.

"Your mother is free to do whatever she pleases," he said unconvincingly.

"The only one she pleases is you," Maribeth said defiantly, making him angrier still, "and you know that."

"I only know that you've disgraced us all. Don't expect to yell at me, and do whatever you want, dishonor all of us, and bring your bastard here. Don't expect anything from me, Maribeth, until you pay for your sins, and clean up your own mess. If you won't marry this boy, and he won't marry you, then there's nothing I can do for you." He turned then and walked out of the room and came back five minutes later. She hadn't even had the strength to go back to her own room yet. He had made two calls, one to their doctor and the other to the convent. Eight hundred dollars would pay for room and board and her expenses for six months, as well as her delivery by the nuns. They assured Mr. Robertson that his daughter would be in good hands,

84

her delivery would be handled right in their infirmary, by a doctor and a midwife. And the baby would be given to a loving family, and his own daughter would be returned to him a week after the baby's birth, providing there were no complications.

He had already agreed to send her to them, and the money was in crisp bills in a white envelope, which he handed to her with a stony look on his face. Her mother had already retreated in tears to her own bedroom.

"You've upset your mother terribly," he said in a voice filled with accusation, denying any part he may have played in the upset. "I don't want you to say anything to Noelle. You're going away. That's all she needs to know. You'll be back in six months. I'll take you to the convent myself tomorrow morning. Pack your bags, Maribeth." The tone of his voice told her he meant business, and she felt her blood run cold. For all her problems with him, this was home, this was her family, these were her parents, and now she was being banished from all of them. She would have no one to help her through this. She wondered suddenly if she should have made a bigger fuss with Paul, if maybe then he would have helped her . . . or maybe even married her instead of Debbie. But it was too late now. Her father was telling her to leave. He wanted her out by the next morning.

"What'll I tell Noelle?" Maribeth could hardly squeeze the words out. She was breathless with the grief of leaving her little sister.

"Tell her you're going away to school. Tell her anything but the truth. She's too young to know about this." Maribeth nodded, numb finally, too grief-stricken even to answer.

Maribeth went back to their bedroom then, and avoided Noelle's eyes as she got down her only bag. She only packed a few things, some shirts, some pants, a few dresses that would fit for a while. She hoped the nuns would give her something to wear. In a little while nothing would fit her.

"What are you doing?" Noelle asked, looking panicked. She had tried to listen to their arguing, but she couldn't make out what they were saying. But Maribeth looked as though someone had died as she turned, trembling, to face her baby sister.

"I'm going away for a while," Maribeth said sadly, wanting to tell her a convincing lie, but it was all too much, too hard, too sudden. She couldn't bear the thought of saying goodbye, and she could hardly withstand the battering of Noelle's questions. In the end, she told her that she was going away somewhere, to a special school, because her grades hadn't been as good as usual, but Noelle only clung to her and cried, terrified to lose her only sister.

"Please don't go . . . don't let him send you away . . . whatever you did, it can't be that terrible . . . whatever it is, Maribeth, I forgive you . . . I love you . . . don't go . . ." Maribeth was the only one Noelle could talk to. Her mother was too weak, her father too stubborn to ever listen, her brother too self-centered and too foolish. She only had Maribeth to listen to her problems, and now she would have no one at all. Poor little Noelle looked miserable as the two sisters cried through the night, and slept in one narrow bed, clinging to each other. And the morning came too soon. At nine o'clock, her father put her bag into his truck, and she stood staring at her mother, wanting her to be strong enough to tell him he couldn't do this. But her mother would never challenge him, and Maribeth knew it. She held her close for a long moment, wishing that she could stay, that she hadn't been so foolish, or so unlucky.

"I love you, Mom," she said in a strangled voice as her mother hugged her tight.

"I'll come to see you, Maribeth, I promise."

Maribeth could only nod, unable to speak through her tears, as she held Noelle, who was crying openly, and begging her not to leave them.

"Shhh . . . stop . . ." Maribeth said, trying to be brave, as she cried too. "I won't be gone long. I'll be home by Christmas."

"I love you, Maribeth," Noelle shouted as they drove away. Ryan had come out by then too. But he had said nothing. He only waved, as his father drove her the short distance across town to their destination.

The convent looked ominous to Maribeth as

they drove up to it, and he stood next to her on the steps as she held her small suitcase.

"Take care of yourself, Maribeth." She didn't want to thank him for what he'd done. It could have been gentler, he could have tried to understand. He could have tried to remember what it was like to be young, or to make a mistake of such monumental proportions, but he was capable of none of it. He could not grow beyond what he was, and what he was had powerful limitations.

"I'll write to you, Dad," she said, but he said nothing to her as they stood there for a long moment, and then he nodded.

"Let your mother know how you are. She'll worry." She wanted to ask him if he would worry too, but she no longer dared ask him any questions.

"I love you," she said softly as he hurried down the steps, but he never turned to look at her. He only lifted one hand as he drove away, and never looked back, and Maribeth rang the bell at the convent.

The wait seemed so long that she wanted to run down the steps and back home, but there was no home to run back to now. She knew they wouldn't take her back until after it was all over. And then, at last, a young nun came, and let her in. Maribeth told her who she was, and with a nod, the young nun took her bag, led her in, and closed the heavy iron door resoundingly behind her.

Chapter Three

The convent of the Sisters of Charity was a cavernous, dark, gloomy place, and Maribeth discovered very quickly that there were two other girls there for exactly the same reason. Both were from neighboring towns, and she was relieved to realize that she didn't know them. Both were almost ready to give birth, and in fact one of them, a nervous girl of seventeen, had her baby on Maribeth's second day there. She had a little girl, and the baby was quickly spirited away to waiting adoptive parents. The girl never even saw her baby. And to Maribeth, the entire process seemed barbaric, as if their secret was dirty and had to be hidden.

The other girl was fifteen, and she was expecting her baby to be born at any moment. The two girls ate their meals with the nuns, went to the chapel with them for prayers and vespers, and were only allowed to speak at certain times and hours. And Maribeth was shocked to discover on her third night that the other girl's baby had been fathered by her uncle. She was a desperately unhappy girl, and she was terrified of what lay ahead of her in childbirth.

On Maribeth's fifth night in the convent, she could hear the other girl's screams. They went on for two days as the nuns scurried everywhere, and at last she was taken to a hospital and de-livered by cesarean section. Maribeth was told, when she inquired, that the girl would not come back again, but the baby had been born safely, and she learned only by coincidence that it was a little boy. It was even lonelier for her once both of the other girls were gone, and Maribeth was alone with the sisters. She hoped that other sinners would arrive soon, or she would have no one to talk to.

She read the local newspaper whenever she could, and two weeks after she'd arrived she saw the notice of Paul and Debbie's wedding. It made her feel even lonelier, just seeing that, knowing they were on their honeymoon, and she was here in prison, paying her dues for one night in the front seat of his Chevy. It seemed des-perately unfair that she should bear the brunt alone, and the more she thought of it, the more she knew that she couldn't stay at the convent.

She had nowhere to go, and no one to be with. But she couldn't bear the oppressive sanc-tity of the convent. The nuns had been pleasant to her, and she had already paid them a hundred dollars. She had seven hundred dollars left, and almost six months to be wherever she went. She had no idea where to go, but she knew she couldn't stay locked up with them, waiting for other prisoners like her to arrive, for the months to pass, for her baby to be born, and then taken away from her, before she could go home to her parents. Being there was too high a price to pay.

She wanted to go somewhere, live like a real person, get a job, have friends. She needed fresh air, and voices, and noise, and people. Here, all she felt was constant oppression, and the over-whelming sense that she was an unredeemable sinner. And even if she was, she needed a little sunshine and joy in her life while she waited for the baby. She didn't know why this had happened to her, but perhaps there was a lesson to learn, a blessing to be shared, a moment in time that need not be wasted. It didn't have to be as terrible as the nuns made it, and she told the Mother Superior the following afternoon that she would be leaving. She said she was going to visit her aunt and hoped that she believed her. But even if she didn't, Maribeth knew that nothing could stop her now, she was leaving.

She walked out of the convent at dawn the next day, with her money, and her small bag, and an overwhelming feeling of freedom. She couldn't go home, but the world was her own, to discover, to explore. She had never felt as free or as strong. She had already been through enormous pain when she left home, and now it was only a matter of finding a place to stay until the baby was born. She knew it would be easier if she left town, so she walked to the bus station and bought an open-ended ticket to Chicago. She had to go through Omaha, but Chicago was the farthest point she could imagine, and she could refund the rest of the ticket anywhere along the way. All she wanted to do was leave, and find a place for herself for the next six months until she had her baby. She waited at the bus station until the first bus to Chicago began to board. And as she watched her hometown slip away, when it left, she felt no regrets. All she felt suddenly was excitement about the future. The past held little for her, just like her hometown. She had no friends there. There was no one she would miss except her mother and her sister. She had written them each a postcard from the bus station, before she left, promising to give them an address as soon as she had one.

"Going to Chicago, miss?" the driver asked, as she sat down, feeling suddenly grown up, and very independent.

"Maybe," she said with a smile. She could go anywhere, and do anything. She was free. She answered to no one now, except herself, fettered only by the baby growing inside her. She was three and a half months pregnant now, and nothing showed, but she could feel her body growing. She began thinking about what she would tell people wherever she arrived. She'd have to explain how she got there, and why she'd come, and why she was alone, once they discovered she was pregnant. She would have to get a job. There wasn't much she could do. But she could clean house, work in a library, baby-sit, maybe work as a waitress. She was willing to do almost anything as long as she was safe. And until she found a job, she still had the money her father had given her for the convent.

They stopped in Omaha that afternoon. It was hot, but there was a slight breeze, and she felt a little sick from the long ride on the bus, but she felt better after she ate a sandwich. Other people got on and off, and most of them seemed to ride from one town to the next. She had been on the longest when they stopped that night in a picturesque little town that looked clean and pretty. It was a college town, and there were lots of young people in the restaurant where they stopped for dinner. It reminded Maribeth a little bit of a diner, but it was nicer than that, and the woman who waited on her had a dark well-tended pageboy, and a big smile as she served Maribeth a cheeseburger and a milkshake. The hamburger was great, and the check was small, and there seemed to be a lot of laughter and good spirits coming from several of the other tables. It seemed like a happy place, and Maribeth was reluctant to leave and go back to the bus, but they were riding straight through en route to Chicago. As she left the restaurant, she saw it. A small sign in the window offering work to waitresses and busboys. She looked at it for a minute, and then walked slowly back, wondering if they'd think she was crazy, or if they'd believe whatever story she invented.

The same waitress who had waited on her looked up at her with a smile, wondering if she'd forgotten something. Maribeth seemed to be hesitating as she stood there and waited.

"I was wondering if . . . I . . . I saw the sign

". . . I was wondering about the job. I mean . . ."

"You mean you want work," the other woman smiled. "No shame in that. It pays two dollars an hour. Six days a week, ten-hour days. We kind of rotate our schedules, so we get a little time home with our kids. You married?"

"No . . . I . . . yes . . . well, I was. I'm a widow. My husband was killed in . . . Korea . . ."

"I'm sorry." She genuinely seemed to mean it, as she watched Maribeth's eyes. She could see that the girl really wanted the job, and she liked her. She looked awfully young, but there was no harm in that, so were a lot of their patrons.

"Thank you . . . who do I talk to about the job?"

"Me. You got any experience?" Maribeth hesitated, toying with a lie, and then she shook her head, wondering if she should tell her about the baby.

"I really need the job." Her hands were shaking as she held her handbag, hoping she would get it. Suddenly she wanted to stay here. It felt like a happy place, a lively town, and she liked it.

"Where do you live?"

"Nowhere yet." She smiled, looking very young, and it tugged at the other woman's heart. "I just came through on the bus. If you want me, I'll get my bag and find a room. I could start tomorrow." The other woman smiled. Her name was Julie, and she liked Maribeth's looks. There was something strong and quiet about the girl, as though she had principles and courage. It was an odd thing to guess about her, and yet she had a good feeling about her.

"Go get your bag off the bus," Julie said with a warm smile, "you can stay with me tonight. My son's visiting my mom in Duluth. You can have his room, if you can stand the mess. He's fourteen and a real slob. My daughter's twelve. I'm divorced. How old are you?" she asked, almost all in one breath, and Maribeth spoke over her shoulder, and told her she was eighteen, as she ran to get her bag off the bus, and came back only two minutes later, breathless and smiling.

"You're sure it's not too much trouble if I spend the night with you?" She was excited and happy.

"Not at all." Julie grinned as she tossed her an apron. "Here, get to work. You can bus tables with me till I knock off at midnight." It was only an hour and a half away, but it was exhausting work, carrying the big trays, and heavy pitchers. Maribeth couldn't believe how tired she was when they closed up. There were four other women working there, and some young boys, mostly high school kids, busing tables. Most of the boys were about Maribeth's age, and the women were in their thirties and forties. They said the owner had had a heart attack and only came in mornings and some afternoons

95

now. But he ran a tight ship, and his son did most of the cooking. Julie said she had gone out with him a few times, and he was a nice guy, but nothing much had ever come of it. She had too much responsibility in her life to have much interest or time for romance. She had two kids, and her ex-husband was five years late with his child support. She said it took every penny she had to keep her kids in shoes, pay their doctor bills, and keep their teeth from falling out of their heads, not to mention all the other things they wanted or needed.

"Bringing up kids on your own is no joke," she said seriously as she drove Maribeth home with her. "They ought to explain that to you real well before you get divorced. Kids aren't made to have alone, let me tell you. You get a headache, you get sick, you're tired, no one cares, you're all they've got. It all ends up on your shoulders. I don't have family here . . . the girls at the restaurant are real nice about helping me out. They baby-sit, they let me drop the kids off if I have a big date. One of the guys, Martha's husband, he takes my boy out to fish every chance he gets. That kind of stuff means a lot. You can't do it all alone. God knows I try. Sometimes I think it's gonna kill me."

Maribeth was listening carefully, and the wisdom of Julie's words wasn't lost on her. Once again, she found herself wanting to tell Julie about the baby, but she didn't.

"Too bad you and your husband didn't have

kids," Julie said gently, as if she were reading her thoughts. "But you're young. You'll get married again. How old were you when you got married anyway?"

"Seventeen. Right out of high school. We were only married a year."

"That's real bad luck, honey." She patted the young girl's hand and parked her car in the driveway. She lived in a small apartment in the rear, and her little girl was sound asleep when Julie let them in. "I hate leaving her alone, and usually her brother is here. The neighbors listen for her, and she's real independent. She comes to the restaurant with me sometimes too, if I really get stuck. But they don't like it." It was a good view of what it was like to take care of kids alone, and she didn't make it sound easy. She'd been alone for ten years, ever since the kids were two and four, and she'd moved around a bit, but she liked it here and she thought Maribeth would too. "It's a nice little town, lots of decent kids, and good people working at the college. We see a lot of them at Jimmy D's, and lots of kids. They're gonna love you."

She showed Maribeth where the bathroom was, and her son's room. His name was Jeffrey and he was gone for two weeks. Julie said Maribeth could stay with them till she found a room. If need be, she'd have her daughter sleep with her once Jeff got back, and give her Jessica's room, but with all the student quarters available, she was sure she'd find something soon.

And she was right. By noon the next day, Maribeth had found an adorable little room in someone's house. It was all done in flowery pink chintzes, and it was a tiny room, but it was cozy and flooded with sunlight, and the price was reasonable. And it was only six blocks away from Jimmy D's, where she would be working. It felt as though everything was falling into place for her. She had only been in town for a few hours, but she felt happy here. It was as though she knew she was meant to be here.

She dropped her parents a postcard on the way to work, with her address, and as she did, she thought about Paul again, and knew there was no point thinking about him. She wondered for how much of her life she would think of him, wondering what he was doing, and where their child was.

At Jimmy D's that day, one of the other waitresses gave her a pink uniform with little white cuffs, and a clean white apron. And she started taking orders that afternoon. Lots of the guys seemed to look at her, and she knew the cook did too, but no one said anything they shouldn't. Everyone was friendly and polite, and she knew that all of the other women had whispered it around that she was a widow. They believed her too. It never occurred to any of them not to.

"How's it going, kid?" Julie asked late that afternoon, impressed with her. She had worked hard, and was pleasant to everyone, and it was easy to see that the customers liked her. A few of them asked her name, and some of the younger customers really seemed to enjoy her. And Jimmy liked her too. He had come in that day, and liked what he saw. She was smart, she was neat, and he could tell from looking at her, he said, that she was honest. She was pretty too, and he liked that in a restaurant. No one wanted to look at a sour old bag, who slammed the coffee down in front of the customers and didn't really want to be there. Jimmy wanted all his waitresses, young or old, to be smiling and happy. He wanted them to make people feel good. Like Julie and the others. And now Maribeth. She made a real effort, and she liked the job. She was thrilled to be there.

But Maribeth was exhausted when she walked home to her new room that night, reminding herself of how lucky she was to have found a job, and a room. Now she could go on with her life. She could even take books out from the library, and continue with her studies. She wasn't going to let this ruin her life. She had already decided that. These months were just a detour for her, but she was determined not to lose her way or her direction.

She was waiting on tables the next night, when a serious young man came in, and ordered meat loaf. Julie said he came in frequently for dinner.

"I don't know why," she said knowingly, "but I get the feeling he doesn't like to go home. He doesn't talk, he doesn't smile. But he's always polite. He's a nice kid. I always want to ask him what he's doing here, instead of going home to dinner. Maybe he has no mom. Something happened there. He's got the saddest eyes I've ever seen. Why don't you go wait on him and make his day." She gave Maribeth a little push in his direction, down toward his end of the counter. He had only looked at the menu for a minute or two before deciding. He had already tried just about everything they had, and he had certain favorites he always liked to order.

"Hi. What would you like?" Maribeth asked shyly, as he glanced at her in covert admiration.

"The number two, thanks. Meat loaf and mashed potatoes." He blushed. He liked her red hair and tried not to stare at her figure.

"Salad, corn, or spinach?" She remained non-committal.

"Corn, thanks," he said, eyeing her. He knew he hadn't seen her there before, and he came in often. He had dinner there three or four times a week, sometimes even on weekends. Their food was plentiful and good and cheap. And when his mother stopped cooking it was the only way he could get a decent dinner.

"Coffee?"

"No, milk. And apple pie à la mode for dessert," he said, as if he was afraid it might run out, and she smiled.

"How do you know you'll have room? We serve pretty big portions."

"I know," he smiled back. "I eat here all the time. You're new, aren't you?" She nodded, feel-

100

ing shy for the first time since she'd been there. He was a nice kid, and she suspected he was about her own age, and somehow she got the impression that he knew it.

"Yeah, I'm new. I just moved here."

"What's your name?" He was very direct, and very honest. But Julie was right, there was something devastating in his eyes. It almost made you afraid to look there, except that you knew you had to. Something about him drew Maribeth to him. It was as though she had to see who he was and know more about him.

"My name's Maribeth."

"I'm Tom. It's nice to meet you."

"Thanks." She went off to order his dinner for him then, and came back with his glass of milk. Julie had already teased her by then, and said he had never spoken as much to anyone since he'd been there.

"Where are you from?" he asked when she came back, and she told him. "What made you move here, or should I ask?"

"A lot of things. I like it here. The people are really nice. The restaurant's great. I found a real pretty little room near here. Everything just kind of worked out." She smiled, and was surprised at how easy it was to talk to him. And when she came back with his dinner, he seemed more interested in talking to her than eating.

He nibbled at his pie for a long time, and ordered another piece and another glass of milk, which he had never done before, and talked to her a lot about fly-fishing nearby and asked if she'd ever done it.

She had, a number of years before with her father and brother, but she'd never been very good at it. She liked just sitting there, while they fished, and reading or thinking.

"You could come with me sometime," he said, and then blushed, wondering why he was talking to her so much. He hadn't been able to take his eyes off her since he'd walked into the restaurant and first seen her.

He left her a big tip, and then stood awk-wardly for a moment on his side of the counter. "Well, thanks for everything. See you again next time." And then he walked out. She noticed how tall he was, and how lanky and thin. He was good-looking, but he didn't seem to know it. And he seemed very young. He seemed more like a brother than a boy she'd have been inter-ested in, but whatever he was, or would be, or even if she never saw him again, he'd been nice to talk to.

He came in again the next day, and the day after that, and he was deeply disappointed to find that she had a day off and he missed her. And then he came back again after the weekend.

"I missed you last time," he said as he ordered fried chicken. He had a healthy appetite, and he always ordered a whole dinner. He seemed to spend most of his paper route money on food. He ate out a lot, and Maribeth wondered if he lived with his parents, and she finally asked him.

"Do you live alone?" she asked cautiously, as she set his meal down and refilled his glass of milk. She didn't write it on the check. They gave free coffee refills after all, it wouldn't break Jimmy to pay for a glass of milk for a regular patron like Tommy.

"Not really. I live with my parents. But . . . they . . . uh . . . everyone kind of does their own thing. And my mom doesn't like to cook anymore. She's going back to work this fall. She's a teacher. She's been subbing for a long time, but she's going back full-time at the high school."

"What does she teach?"

"English, social studies, lit. She's pretty good. She's always giving me extra work to do," he said, rolling his eyes, but he didn't really look as though he minded.

"You're lucky. I've had to take some time off from school, and I know I'm really going to miss it."

"College or high school?" he asked with interest. He was still trying to peg her age. She seemed older than her years, and yet in some ways, he got the feeling she was closer to his own age. She hesitated for only a moment before answering.

"High school." He figured she was probably a senior. "I'm going to be doing some work on my own, until I go back after Christmas." She said it defensively, and he wondered why she had dropped out, but he decided not to ask her.

"I can lend you some books, if you want. I can even get some stuff from my mom, she'd love it. She thinks the whole world should be doing independent studies. Do you like school?" He could see from the look in her eyes that she was being honest with him when she nodded. There was a real hunger there, an appetite that was never completely sated. On her day off she had gone to the library to borrow books that would help her keep up with her own classes.

"What do you like best?" she asked, clearing his plates. He had ordered blueberry pie à la mode for dessert. It was the pie they did best, and he loved it.

"English," he answered as she set his pie down, and felt her back ache. But she liked standing there talking to him. They always seemed to have so much to say to each other. "English lit, English comp. Sometimes I think I might like to write. My mom would probably like that. My dad expects me to go into the business."

"What kind of business is that?" she asked, intrigued by him. He was a smart, good-looking kid, and yet he seemed so lonely. He never came in with friends, never seemed to want to go home. She wondered about him, and why he seemed so alone, and so lonely.

"He's in produce," he explained. "My grandfather started it. They used to be farmers. But then they started selling produce from all over. It's pretty interesting, but I like writing better.

I might like to teach, like my mom." He shrugged then, looking very young again. He liked talking to her, and he didn't mind answering her questions. He had a few of his own, but he decided to save them. And before he left that night, he asked when she was going to be off again.

"Friday."

He nodded, wondering if she'd be shocked if he asked her to go for a walk with him, or to the swimming hole outside town. "Would you like to do something Friday afternoon? I have to help my dad in the morning. But I could pick you up around two. He'll let me have the truck. We could go to the swimming hole, or out to the lake. We can go fishing if you want." He looked desperately hopeful as he waited.

"I'd like that. Whatever you want to do." She lowered her voice then, so the others wouldn't hear, and gave him her address, and she didn't hesitate for a minute. He looked like the kind of person you could trust, and she felt completely at ease with him. She knew instinctively just from talking to him that Tommy Whittaker was her friend, and he would do nothing to harm her.

"Did you just make a date with him?" Julie asked with a curious grin when he left. One of the other girls thought she had heard him invite Maribeth to go fishing, and they were all giggling and laughing and speculating. She was such a kid, but they all liked her. And they liked him.

He had been a mystery to them ever since he'd started coming in the previous winter. He never said anything to them, he just came in and ordered dinner. But with Maribeth, he had really come alive and he never seemed to stop talking.

"Of course not," she said in answer to Julie's question. "I don't date customers," she said pointedly, and Julie didn't believe her for a minute.

"You can do anything you want, you know. Jimmy doesn't mind. He's a cute kid, and he really likes you."

"He's just a friend, that's all. He says his mom hates to cook so he comes in here for dinner."

"Well, he certainly told you his life story, didn't he now."

"Oh for heaven's sake." Maribeth grinned, and walked into the kitchen to pick up a tray of hamburgers for a bunch of students. But as she walked back with the heavy tray, she smiled to herself, thinking of Friday.

Chapter Four

On Friday, his father let him leave work at eleven o'clock, and he picked her up at eleven-thirty. Maribeth was waiting for him in an old pair of jeans and saddle shoes and a big shirt that had been her father's. The jeans were rolled up almost to her knees, and she was wearing her bright red hair in pigtails. She looked about fourteen, and the big shirt concealed her growing paunch. She hadn't been able to zip her jeans up for weeks now.

"Hi, I finished earlier than I thought I would. I told my dad I was going fishing. He thought it was a great idea and told me to get going." He helped her into the truck, and they stopped at a small market on the way to buy some sandwiches for lunch. Tommy ordered roast beef, and she had tuna. They were big homemade-looking sandwiches, and they bought a six-pack of Cokes, and a box of cookies.

"Anything else?" Tommy asked, excited just being with her. She was so pretty and so alive, and there was something very grown up about her. Not living at home, and having a job, somehow made her seem very mature and a lot older.

Maribeth picked up a couple of apples and a Hershey bar, and Tommy insisted on paying. She tried to split the expense with him, but he wouldn't let her. He was long and tall and lean as he followed her back to the truck, carrying their groceries and admiring her figure.

"So how come you left home so young?" he asked as they drove to the lake. He hadn't heard the story yet about her being a widow. He figured maybe her parents had died, or something dramatic had happened. Most kids their age didn't just drop out of school and move away. Something about her suggested to him that there was more to the story.

"I . . . uh . . . I don't know." She glanced out the window for a long time, and then back at him. "It's kind of a long story." She shrugged, thinking about what it had been like leaving home and moving to the convent. It had been the most depressing place she'd ever been, and she was glad every day she hadn't stayed there. At least here she felt alive, she had a job, she was taking care of herself, and now she had met him. Maybe they could be friends. She was beginning to feel she had a life here. She had called home a couple of times, but her mom just cried, and they wouldn't let her speak to Noelle. And the last time she called, her mother said that maybe it would be better if she wrote and didn't call them. They were happy to know that she was well, and doing all right, but her father was still very angry at her, and he said he wouldn't talk to her until after "her problem was taken care of." Her mother kept referring to the baby as Maribeth's "problem."

Maribeth sighed, thinking of all that, and then looked at Tommy. He had nice clean-cut looks, and he seemed like a good person to talk to. "We had a big fight and my father made me move out. He wanted me to stay in our hometown, but after a couple of weeks I just decided that I couldn't. So I came here, and got a job." She made it all sound so simple, with none of the agony it had caused her, the terror, or the heartbreak.

"But you're going back?" He looked confused, she had already told him she was going back to school after Christmas.

"Yeah. I've got to get back to school," she said matter-of-factly, as the road curved lazily toward the lake. His fishing pole was in the truck behind them.

"Why don't you go here?"

"I can't," she said, not wanting to elaborate further. And then to change the subject for a little while, she looked at him, wondering what his family was like, and why he never seemed to want to be with them.

"Do you have brothers and sisters?" she asked casually, as they arrived, realizing again how little she knew about him. He turned off the engine, and looked at her, and for a long moment there was silence.

"I did," he said quietly. "Annie. She was five. She died just after Christmas." He got out of the truck then, without saying anything more, and went to get his fishing pole as Maribeth watched him, wondering if that was the pain one saw so easily in his eyes, if that was why he never went home to his parents.

She got out of the truck, and followed him to the lake. They found a quiet spot at the end of a sandy beach and he slipped off his jeans. He had bathing trunks on, and he unbuttoned his shirt as she watched him. For the flash of an instant, she thought of Paul, but there was no similarity between them. None. Paul was sophisticated and smooth, and very much the man-about-campus. He was also married by then, and he was part of another life. Everything about Tommy was wholesome and pure. He seemed very innocent, and incredibly nice, and she was startled by how much she liked him.

She sat down on the sand next to him, while he baited his hook.

"What was she like?" Her voice was very soft, and he didn't look up from what he was doing.

"Annie?" He looked up at the sun, and then closed his eyes for a second before glancing at Maribeth. He didn't want to talk about it, and yet with her he felt as if he could. He knew they were going to be friends but he wanted more than that from her. She had great legs, and great eyes, a smile that melted him, and a sensational figure. But he wanted to be her friend too. He wanted to do things for her, to be there for her when she needed a friend, and he sensed that she did now, although he wasn't sure why. But there was something very vulnerable about her.

"She was the sweetest kid that ever lived, big blue eyes, and white-blond hair. She looked like the little angel on top of the Christmas tree . . . and sometimes she was a little devil. She used to tease me, and follow me everywhere. We made a big snowman right before she died. . . ." His eyes filled with tears and he shook his head. It was the first time he had ever talked about her to anyone, and it was hard for him. Maribeth could see that. "I really miss her," he admitted in a voice that was barely more than a croak, as Maribeth touched his arm with gentle fingers.

"It's okay to cry . . . I'll bet you miss her a lot. Was she sick for a long time?"

"Two days. We thought she just had influenza, or a cold or something. It was meningitis. They couldn't do anything. She just went. I kept thinking it should have been me afterwards. I mean, why her? Why a little tiny kid like that? She was only five years old, she never did anything to hurt anyone, she never did anything but make us happy. I was ten when she was born, and she was so funny and soft and warm and cuddly, like a little puppy." He smiled, thinking about her, and moved closer to Maribeth on the warm sand, laying his pole down beside him. In a funny way, it felt good talking about her now, as though it brought her back to him for the briefest of moments. He never talked to anyone about her anymore. No one ever brought her up, and he knew he couldn't say anything to his parents.

"Your parents must have taken it pretty hard," Maribeth said, wise beyond her years, and almost as though she knew them.

"Yeah. Everything kind of stopped when she died. My parents stopped talking to each other, or even to me. No one says anything, or goes anywhere. No one smiles. They never talk about her. They never talk about anything. Mom hardly ever cooks anymore, Dad never comes home from work till ten o'clock. It's like none of us can stand being in the house without her. Mom's going back to work full-time in the fall. It's like everyone's given up because she's gone. She didn't just die, we did too. I hate being home now. It's so dark and depressing. I hate walking past her room, everything seems so empty." Maribeth just listened to him, she had slipped her hand into his, and they were looking out over the lake together.

"Do you ever feel her there with you, like when you think about her?" she asked, feeling his pain with him, and almost feeling as though she knew her. She could almost see the beautiful little girl he had loved so much, and feel how devastated he had been when he lost her.

"Sometimes. I talk to her sometimes, late at night. It's probably a dumb thing to do, but sometimes I feel like she can hear me." Maribeth nodded, she had talked to her grandmother that way after she died, and it had made her feel better.

"I'll bet she can hear you, Tommy. I'll bet

she watches you all the time. Maybe she's happy now . . . maybe some people just aren't meant to be in our lives forever. Maybe some people are just passing through . . . maybe they get it all done faster than the rest of us. They don't need to stick around for a hundred years to get it all right. They get it down real quick . . . it's like . . ." She struggled to find the right words to tell him, but it was something she had thought about a lot, especially lately. "It's like some people just come through our lives to bring us something, a gift, a blessing, a lesson we need to learn, and that's why they're here. She taught you something, I'll bet . . . about love, and giving, and caring so much about someone . . . that was her gift to you. She taught you all that, and then she left. Maybe she just didn't need to stay longer than that. She gave you the gift, and then she was free to move on . . . she was a special soul . . . you'll have that gift forever."

He nodded, trying to absorb all that she'd said to him. It made sense, more or less, but it still hurt so damn much. But it felt better talking to Maribeth. It was as though she really understood what he'd been through.

"I wish she could have stayed longer," he said with a sigh. "I wish you could have met her." And then he smiled. "She would have had a lot to say about whether or not I liked you, who you were prettier than, and whether or not you liked me. She was always volunteering her opinions. Most of the time, she drove me crazy."

Maribeth laughed at the thought, wishing she could have met her. But then maybe she wouldn't have met him. He wouldn't have been going to the restaurant to eat three or four times a week, he'd have been home with his family, having dinner.

"What would she have said about us?" Maribeth teased, liking the game, liking him, comfortable sitting on the sand near him. She had learned some hard lessons in the past few months about who to trust, and who not to, and she had sworn she would never trust anyone again, but she knew to the bottom of her very soul that Tommy Whittaker was different.

"She'd have said I like you." He grinned, looking sheepish, and she noticed freckles on the bridge of his nose for the first time. They were tiny and almost golden in the bright sunlight. "She'd have been right too. Usually she wasn't." But Annie would have sensed immediately how much he liked her. Maribeth was more mature than the girls he knew at school, and the most beautiful girl he'd ever seen. "I think she would really have liked you." He smiled gently, and lay back on the sand, looking at Maribeth with unconcealed admiration. "What about you? You have a boyfriend back home?" He decided to ask her now so he'd know where things stood, and she hesitated for a moment. She thought about telling him the fiction of the young husband in the Korean war, but she just couldn't. She'd explain it to

114

him later on, if she still had to.

"Nope. Not really."

"But sort of?"

She shook her head firmly this time in answer. "I went out with one guy I thought I liked, but I was wrong. And anyway, he just got married."

He looked intrigued. An older man. "Do you care? That he's married, I mean?"

"Not really." All she cared about was that he had left her with a baby. A baby she couldn't keep, and didn't really want. She cared about that a lot, but said nothing about it to Tommy.

"How old are you, by the way?"

"Sixteen," and then they discovered that their birthdays were only weeks apart. They were exactly the same age, but their situations were very different. However useless to him they were at the moment, he was still part of a family, he had a home, he was going back to school in the fall. She had none of those things anymore, and in less than five months she was having a baby, the baby of a man who had never loved her. It was overwhelmingly scary.

He walked out into the lake after a little while, and she went with him. They stood together while he fished, and when he finally got bored, he walked back to the shore and left his fishing pole, and dived into the water, but she didn't join him. She waited for him on the sand, and when he came out, he asked her why she hadn't gone swimming. It was a hot sunny day and the cool water felt good on his flesh. She would have loved to swim with him, but she didn't want him to see her bulging belly. She kept her father's shirt on the entire time, and only slipped her jeans off while they stood in the water.

"Can you swim?" he asked, and she laughed, feeling silly.

"Yeah, I just didn't feel like it today. I always feel a little creepy swimming in lakes, you never know what's in the water with you."

"That's dumb. Why don't you go in? There aren't even any fish, you saw I couldn't catch one."

"Maybe next time," she said, drawing designs in the sand with her fingers. They ate lunch sitting in the shade of an enormous tree, and talked about their families and their childhoods. She told him about Ryan and Noelle, and how her father thought that sons should get everything, and girls didn't need to do anything except get married and have kids. She told him about how she wanted to be something one day, like a teacher or a lawyer, or a writer, how she didn't want to just get married and have kids straight out of high school.

"You sound just like my mom," he smiled. "She made my dad wait for six years after she finished high school. She went to college and got her degree, and then she taught for two years, and after that they got married. And then it took her seven years to have me, and another ten to have Annie. I think they had a really hard time having kids. But education is really important to my mom. She says the only valuable things you've got are your mind, and your education."

"I wish my mom felt like that. She does everything my dad tells her to. She thinks girls don't need to go to college. My parents don't want me to go. They would have let Ryan, probably, if he'd wanted to, but he just wanted to work in the shop with my dad. He'd have gone to Korea, except he was 4-F, but Dad says he's a great mechanic. You know," she tried to explain things to him she had never said to anyone before, "I always felt different from them. I've always wanted things no one else in my family cares about. I want to go to school, I want to learn a lot of things, I want to be really smart. I don't just want to catch some guy, and have a bunch of kids. I want to make something of myself. Everyone I know just thinks I'm crazy." But he didn't, and she sensed that, he came from a family that felt exactly the way she did. It was as though she had been dropped off at the wrong place when she was born, and had been doomed to a lifetime of misunderstandings. "I think my sister will do what they want in the end. She complains, but she's a good kid. She's thirteen, but she's already boy crazy." On the other hand, Noelle hadn't gotten pregnant by Paul Browne in the front seat of his car, so Maribeth felt she was in no position to cast aspersions.

"You really ought to talk to my mom some-

117

time, Maribeth. I think you'd like her."

"I'll bet I would." And then she looked at him curiously. "Would she like me? Moms are usually pretty suspicious of the girls their sons like," especially her, in a few months. No, there would be no way she could meet Mrs. Whittaker. In another month she wouldn't be able to hide it anymore, and she wouldn't even want to see Tommy. She hadn't figured out what she would tell him yet, but she would have to tell him something eventually, even if he just came into the restaurant and saw her. She'd have to tell him the story about a young husband dying in Korea, except that now it sounded so stupid. She would have liked to tell him the truth, but she knew she couldn't. It was too terrible, too irresponsible, and much too shocking. She was sure he'd never want to see her again. She'd just have to stop seeing him in a few weeks, and tell him she was seeing someone else. And then he'd be going back to school, and he'd be busy anyway, and he'd probably fall for some high school junior, a cheerleader probably, some perfect girl that his parents knew . . .

"Hey . . . what were you thinking about then?" he interrupted her. She had been a million miles away, thinking of all the cheerleaders he was going to fall in love with. "You looked so sad, Maribeth. Is something wrong?" He knew she had something on her mind, but he had no way of knowing what it was, after they'd known each other for such a short time, but he would have liked to help her.

She had made him feel better about Annie for the first time in months, and he would have liked to return the favor.

"Nothing . . . just daydreaming, I guess . . . there's nothing special . . . ." Just a baby growing inside me, that's all, no biggie.

"Want to go for a walk?" They walked halfway around the lake, sometimes balancing on rocks, sometimes walking through the water, and sometimes across sandy beaches. It was a pretty little lake, and he challenged her to a race on the way back, once they hit a long stretch of beach, but even with her long, graceful legs, she couldn't keep up with him. And they finally collapsed side by side on the sand, and lay there, looking up at the sky, trying to catch their breath and grinning.

"You're pretty good," he conceded, and she laughed. For her, in some ways, it was just like being with a brother.

"I almost caught up with you, except I stumbled on that rock."

"You did not . . . you were miles behind . . . ."

"Yeah, and you started before I did by about eight feet . . . you practically cheated . . . ." She was laughing, and their faces were inches apart, as he looked at her, and admired every single thing about her.

"I did not!" he defended himself, wanting desperately to kiss her.

"Did too . . . I'll beat you next time . . . ."

"Yeah . . . sure . . . I'll bet you can't even swim . . ." He loved teasing her, lying next to her, being with her. He often thought of what it would be like to make love to a woman. He would have liked to know . . . to find out with her . . . but she seemed so womanly and so innocent at the same time that he was afraid to touch her. Instead, he rolled over and lay on his stomach on the sand, so she wouldn't see how much he liked her. And she lay next to him, on her back, and suddenly she got an odd expression. She had felt a twinge, just the oddest feeling, like butterfly wings flapping inside her. The feeling was entirely unfamiliar, but within an instant she knew what it was . . . the first signs of life . . . it was her baby . . .

"You okay?" He was looking down at her, concerned, for a moment she had such a funny look, as though she had been startled, and was distracted.

"Fine," she said softly, suddenly stunned at what had happened as she lay there. It brought it all home to her again, how real the baby was, how alive, how time was moving forward, whether she wanted it to or not. She had thought about going to a doctor to make sure everything was all right, but she didn't know one here, and she couldn't really afford it.

"Sometimes you look a million miles away," he said, wondering what she thought about, when she looked like that. He would have liked to know everything about her.

"Sometimes I just think about things . . . like my folks . . . or my sister . . ."

"Do you talk to them?" He was intrigued, there were still so many little mysteries about her. Everything was new and so exciting.

"I write. It works better that way. My dad still gets kind of mad when I call."

"You must have really made him mad at you."

"It's a long story. I'll tell you one day. Maybe next time." Assuming that there was one.

"When's your next day off?" He couldn't wait to go out with her again. He loved being with her, the scent of her hair, the look in her eyes, the feel of her skin when he held her hand or accidentally touched her, the things she said to him, the ideas they shared. He loved everything about her.

"I've got a couple of hours off on Sunday afternoon. But after that I'm not off again till Wednesday."

"Want to go to a movie Sunday night?" he asked hopefully, and she smiled. No one had ever taken her out like that. Most of the boys at school had no interest in her, except creeps like David O'Connor. She had never really dated anyone . . . not even Paul . . . this was all new to her and she loved it.

"I'd love it."

"I'll pick you up at the restaurant, if that's okay with you. And if you want, Wednesday we could come back here, or we could do something else if you'd rather."

"I love it here," she said, looking around, and then at him, and meant it.

They didn't leave until after six o'clock when the sun started to sink a little lower in the sky, and they drove slowly back to town. He would have liked to take her out to dinner, but he had promised he would help his mother install a new bookcase. And she had insisted she was going to cook dinner, which was rare these days. He had said he would be home by seven.

At twenty to, he was at the little house where Maribeth lived, and she got out of the truck regretfully. She hated to leave him.

"Thanks for a great time." It was the happiest afternoon she'd had in years, and he was the best friend she had ever had. It seemed like providence that he had come into her life now. "I really loved it."

"So did I," he smiled, standing next to her and looking into her shining green eyes. There was a luminous quality about her that mesmerized him. He was dying to kiss her as he stood there. "I'll come by the restaurant tomorrow night for dinner. What time do you get off?"

"Not till midnight," she said regretfully. She would have liked to be free to go everywhere with him, at least for the rest of the summer. After that, everything would change anyway. But just now she could still pretend that it wouldn't. Although, after feeling the baby move that afternoon, she knew that those days were numbered.

"I'll drive you home tomorrow night after

work." His parents didn't mind his going out, and he could tell them he was going to a late movie.

"I'd like that," she smiled at him, and she stood on the front steps and waved as he drove off with a huge smile. He was the happiest boy alive when he got home, and he was still grinning when he walked in the front door of his house at five to seven.

"What happened to you? Did you catch a whale at the lake today?" His mother smiled at him, as she finished setting the table. She had made roast beef, his father's favorite, and Tommy had the odd feeling that she was making a particular effort to please him.

"No . . . no fish . . . just some sun and sand, and a little swimming." The house smelled wonderful, she had made popovers too, and mashed potatoes and sweet corn, everyone's favorites, even Annie's. But the familiar stab of pain at the thought of her seemed a little less acute tonight. Talking about her to Maribeth had helped, and he wished he could share that with his mother, but he knew he couldn't. "Where's Dad?"

"He said he'd be home at six. I guess he got delayed. He'll be home any minute. I told him dinner was at seven." But an hour later, he still hadn't come home, there was no answer when she called him at work, and the roast was well done by then, and her mouth was set in a thin line of fury.

At eight-fifteen she and Tommy ate, and at

nine, his father walked in, obviously having had a few too many drinks, but in very high spirits.

"Well, well, the little woman cooked dinner for a change!" he said jovially, trying to kiss her, but missing even her cheek by several inches. "What's the occasion?"

"You said you'd be home at six o'clock," she said, looking grim, "and I told you I'd have dinner on the table at seven. I just thought it was time this family started having dinner together again." Tommy panicked at her words, but it didn't look as though that was going to happen again anyway, at least not for a while, so he decided not to worry prematurely.

"I guess I forgot. It's been so long since you cooked, I didn't even remember." He looked only mildly apologetic, and made an effort to seem more sober than he was as he sat down at the table. It was rare for him to come home drunk, but his life had been pretty bleak for the past seven months, and relief in the form of a whiskey or two hadn't seemed so bad when offered by two of his employees.

Liz served him up a plate, without saying another word to him, and he looked at it in surprise when she handed it to him.

"The meat's pretty well done, isn't it, dear? You know I like it rare." She grabbed the plate from him then, and poured all the food on it into the garbage can, and then banged the empty plate in the sink with an expression of disappointment.

"Then try coming home before nine o'clock. It was rare two hours ago, John," she said through clenched teeth, and he sat back in his chair, looking deflated.

"Sorry, Liz."

She turned around at the sink then and looked at him, even forgetting that Tommy was there. They always seemed to forget him. It was as though, in their minds, he had left with Annie. His needs no longer seemed to be of importance to anyone. They were too desperately distraught themselves to ever help him.

"I guess it doesn't matter anymore, does it, John? None of it does. None of the little niceties that used to seem so important. We've all given up."

"We don't have to," Tommy said softly. Maribeth had given him hope that afternoon, and if nothing else, he wanted to share it. "We're still here. And Annie would hate what's happened to us. Why don't we try and spend more time with each other again? It doesn't have to be every night, just sometimes."

"Tell your father that," Liz said coldly, and turned her back on them as she started to do the dishes.

"It's too late, Son." His father patted his shoulder and then disappeared into their bedroom.

Liz finished the dishes, and then, tight-lipped, put up the new bookcase with Tommy. She needed it for her schoolbooks in the fall. But she said very little to her son, except about the project they were working on, and then she thanked him and went to the bedroom. It was as though everything about her had changed in the past seven months, all the softness and warmth he had known had hardened to stone, and all he saw in her eyes now was despair, and pain, and sorrow. It was obvious that none of them were going to survive the death of Annie.

John was asleep on the bed with all his clothes on when she walked into the room, and she stood and looked at him for a long moment, and turned and closed the door behind her. Maybe it didn't matter anymore what happened between them. She'd been to the doctor several months before and he had told her there wouldn't be any more children. There wasn't any point even trying. There had been too much damage when Annie was born. And now she was forty-seven years old, and she had always had a hard time getting pregnant, even when she was younger. This time the doctor had admitted to her it was hopeless.

She had no relationship with her husband anymore. He hadn't touched her since the night before Annie died, the night they'd convinced each other all she had was a cold. They still blamed each other and themselves, and the thought of making love to him now repulsed her. She didn't want to make love to anyone, didn't want to be that close to anyone again, didn't want to care about anyone, or love that much, or hurt that much when she lost them. Even John, or Tommy. She was cut off from all of them, she had gone completely cold, and the iciness only masked her pain. John's pain was a lot more blatant. He was in agony. He desperately missed not only his beloved little girl, but his wife, and his son, and there was nowhere to go with what he was feeling, no one he could tell, no one to bring him comfort. He could have cheated on her but he didn't want sex with just anyone, he wanted what they had had before. He wanted the impossible, he wanted their life back.

He stirred as she walked around the room, putting away her things. She went into the bathroom, and put her nightgown on, and then woke him before she turned the lights off.

"Go put your pajamas on," she said, as though she were talking to a child, or perhaps a stranger. She sounded like a nurse, caring for him, not a woman who had once loved him.

He sat on the edge of the bed for a minute, clearing his head, and then he looked up at her. "I'm sorry about tonight, Liz. I guess I just forgot. Maybe I was nervous about coming home and starting all over again. I don't know. I didn't mean to ruin anything." But he had anyway. Life had ruined things for them. She was gone, never to return to them again. They would never ever see their little Annie.

"It doesn't matter," she said, not convincing him or herself. "We'll do it again sometime." But she didn't sound as though she meant it.

"Will you? I'd really like that. I miss your dinners." They had all lost weight that year. It had been a rough seven months for all of them, and it showed. John had aged, and Liz looked gaunt and unhappy, particularly now that she knew for sure there would never be another baby.

He went into the bathroom and put his pajamas on then, and he smelled clean and looked neat when he returned to lie beside her. But she had her back to him, and everything about her felt rigid and unhappy.

"Liz?" he asked in the darkened room. "Do you suppose you'll ever forgive me?"

"There's nothing to forgive. You didn't do anything." Her voice sounded as dead as he felt, and they both looked it.

"Maybe if we had asked the doctor to come that night . . . If I hadn't told you it was just a cold . . ."

"Dr. Stone says it wouldn't have made any difference." But she didn't sound as though she believed it.

"I'm sorry," he said, as tears choked him, and he put a hand on her shoulder. But she didn't move, if anything she seemed even stiffer and more distant from him after he had touched her. "I'm sorry, Liz . . ."

"So am I," she said softly, but she never turned back to him. She never looked at him. She never saw him crying silently in the moonlight, as he lay there, and he never saw her tears sliding slowly into her pillow. They were like two people drowning quietly, in separate oceans.

And as Tommy lay in his bed that night, thinking of them, he figured there was no hope left of ever getting them back together. It was obvious to him that too much had happened to them, the pain was too great, the grief too much to bear or recover from. He had lost not only his sister, but his home, and both his parents. And the only thing that cheered him, as he lay there, thinking about them, was the prospect of seeing Maribeth . . . he thought of the long legs and the bright red hair, the funny old shirt she had worn, and their race on the shores of the lake . . . he thought of a thousand things, and then drifted off to sleep, dreaming of Maribeth walking slowly down the beach at the lake, holding hands with Annie.

Chapter Five

On Sunday, he took her to see *From Here to Eternity* with Burt Lancaster and Deborah Kerr after work, and they both loved it. He sat very close to her, with an arm around her, and they ate popcorn and candy bars, and she cried at all the sad parts, and they both agreed afterwards that it was a great movie.

He drove her home, and they made plans for the following Wednesday afternoon, and she asked him casually how dinner with his parents had been, although she'd seen him in the meantime, she had forgotten to ask him.

"Not so great actually," he said, looking pensive, "actually pretty rotten. My dad forgot to come home. I guess he went out with some guys from work. Anyway, the roast beef got overcooked, my mom got really mad, and my dad came home drunk. Not exactly your perfect evening." He grinned, it was so bad you had to be philosophical about it. "They're pretty mad at each other most of the time. I guess they're just mad at the things they can't change, but they don't seem to be able to help each other."

Maribeth nodded, looking sympathetic, and they sat on her front steps for a while. The old lady who rented the room to her liked to see Maribeth enjoy herself, she really liked her. She told Maribeth all the time that she was too thin, which Maribeth knew would not be the case for long, and in truth wasn't even for the moment. She had already started gaining weight, but she still managed to conceal it, although the apron she wore at work was starting to bulge more than it had in the beginning.

"So what'll we do Wednesday?" Tommy asked happily. "Go back to the lake?"

"Sure. Why don't you let me get the lunch this time? I can even make some stuff here."

"Okay."

"What would you like?"

"Anything you make'll be fine." He just wanted to be with her. And as they sat side by side on the steps, he could feel her body tantalizingly close to his, but still he somehow couldn't manage to lean over and kiss her. Everything about her appealed to him, and just being near her caused him physical pain, but actually taking her in his arms and kissing her was more than he could handle. She could sense his tension as he sat next to her, but she misinterpreted it, and thought it had something to do with his parents.

"Maybe it's just a question of time," she reassured him. "It's only been seven months. Give them a chance. Maybe when your mom goes back to work that'll make things better."

"Or worse," he said, looking worried. "Then she'll never be home. While Annie was alive, she only worked part time. But I guess she figures she doesn't need to be home for me all the time, and she's right. I don't even get home till six o'clock once school starts."

"Do you think they'd ever have another baby?" she asked, looking intrigued, not sure how old they were. But he shook his head. He had wondered the same thing, but he didn't think they would now.

"I think my mom's kind of old for that. She's forty-seven, and she had a lot of trouble having her. I don't even know if they'd want another baby. They never said so."

"Parents don't talk about stuff like that around kids," she grinned, and he looked faintly embarrassed.

"Yeah. I guess not." They made their plans for the following Wednesday afternoon, and he promised to come to dinner at the restaurant either Monday or Tuesday. Julie had figured out that Maribeth was going out with him by then, and they teased her whenever he came in, but it was all in good fun, and they were happy she had someone as nice as Tommy to be friends with.

He said good night to her, standing on one foot, and then the other, feeling awkward with her, which was rare, but he didn't want to move too fast, or too slow, or seem too bold to her, or as though he didn't like her. It was an agonizing moment. And after she gently closed the door, she looked thoughtful as she went upstairs to her bedroom, wondering how, eventually, was she going to tell him the truth about her.

As it turned out, he came to see her at the restaurant the next afternoon, and then came back after work to drive her home for the next two days, and before he picked her up on Wednesday, he went out to the cemetery early that morning, to visit Annie.

He went there from time to time to clean up her grave, and sweep the dead leaves away. There were little flowers that he had planted there, and he always tidied things up. It was something he did just for her, and for his mother, because he knew she worried about it, but couldn't bear to go there.

He talked to her sometimes while he worked, and this time, he told her all about Maribeth, and how much she'd like her. It was as though she were sitting up in a tree somewhere, looking down on him, and he was telling her all about his latest doings.

"She's a great girl . . . no pimples . . . long legs . . . she can't swim, but she's a terrific runner. I think you'd like her." And then he grinned, thinking of both Maribeth and his little sister. In some ways, Maribeth reminded him of the kind of girl Annie might have been if she'd grown up to be sixteen. They had the same kind of straightforward honesty and directness. And the same sense of mischief and good humor.

He finished his work at the gravesite then, thinking about the things Maribeth had said, about some people just passing through one's lives in order to bring a gift, or a special blessing.

133

"Not everyone is meant to stay forever," she had said, and it was the first time that anything had made any sense to him about Annie. Maybe she was just passing through . . . but if only she could have stayed a little longer.

Her little spot in the shade looked all neat and clean again when he left, and it pulled at his heart as it always did, to leave her there and to read her name, Anne Elizabeth Whittaker, on the small tombstone. There was a carving of a little lamb, and it always brought tears to his eyes just to see it.

"Bye kiddo," he whispered just before he left. "I'll be back soon . . . I love you . . ." He still missed her desperately, especially when he came here, and he was quiet when he picked up Maribeth at her house, and she was quick to notice.

"Something wrong?" She glanced at him, she could see that he was upset, and she was instantly worried. "Did something happen?"

"No." He was touched that she had noticed, and he took a minute to answer. "I went out to clean up . . . you know . . . Annie's place at the cemetery today . . . I go there once in a while . . . Mom kind of likes me to, and I like going anyway . . . and I know Mom hates to do it." And then he smiled and glanced over at his friend. She was wearing the big baggy shirt again, but this time with shorts and sandals. "I told her about you. I guess she knows anyway," he said, feeling comfortable with her again. He liked sharing his secrets with her. There was no hesitation, no shame. She was just there, like an extension of him, or someone he had grown up with.

"I had a dream about her the other night," Maribeth said, and he looked startled.

"So did I. I dreamt about the two of you walking at the lake. I just felt so peaceful," he said, and Maribeth nodded.

"I dreamt she was telling me to take care of you, and I promised her I would . . . kind of like a chain of people . . . she left and I came, and she asked me to keep an eye on you . . . and maybe after me someone else . . . and then . . . it's like an eternal progression of people coming through our lives. I think that's what I was trying to say the other day. Nothing is forever, but there's a continuing stream of people who go through our lives and continue with us . . . nothing just stops and stays . . . but it flows on . . . like a river. Does that sound crazy?" She turned to him, wondering if her philosophical meanderings sounded foolish, but they didn't. They were both wise beyond their years, with good reason.

"No, it doesn't. I just don't like the part about the progression of people, coming and going in our lives. I'd like it better if people stayed. I wish Annie were still here, and I don't want 'someone else' after you, Maribeth. What's wrong with staying?"

"We can't always do that," she said, "sometimes we have to move on. Like Annie. We're not always given a choice." But she had a choice, she and her baby were bound to each other for the moment, but eventually Maribeth would move on, and the baby would go on to its own life, in its own world, with other parents. It seemed as though now, in all their lives, nothing was forever.

"I don't like that, Maribeth. At some point, people have to stay."

"Some do. Some don't. Some can't. We just have to love them while we can, and learn whatever we're meant to from them."

"What about us?" he asked, strangely serious for a sixteen-year-old boy. But she was a serious young woman. "Do you suppose we're meant to learn something from each other?"

"Maybe. Maybe we need each other right now," she said wisely.

"You've already taught me a lot about Annie, about letting go, about loving her wherever she is now, and taking her with me."

"You've helped me too," Maribeth said warmly, but not explaining how, and he wondered. And as they drove toward the lake, she felt the baby move again. It had fluttered a number of times since the first time she'd felt it and it was getting to be a familiar and friendly feeling. It was like nothing she'd ever felt before and she liked it.

When they reached the lake, Tommy spread out a blanket he had brought, and Maribeth carried the picnic. She had made egg salad sand-wiches, which he said he loved, and chocolate cake, and brought a bagful of fruit, a bottle of milk, which she seemed to drink a lot of these days, and some sodas. They were both hungry and decided to eat right away, and then they lay on the blanket and talked again for a long time, about school this time, and some of his friends, their parents, and their plans. Tommy said he had been to California once, with his dad, to look at produce there, and Florida for the same reason. She had never been anywhere, and said she'd love to see New York and Chicago. And both of them said they would love to see Europe, but Maribeth thought it unlikely she ever would. She had no way to get anywhere in her life, ex-cept here, and even this had been a great ad-venture for her.

They talked about the Korean war too, and the people they knew who had died. It seemed crazy to both of them that they were engaged in another war so soon after the last one. They both remembered when Pearl Harbor had been hit, they had been four. Tommy's father had been too old to enlist, but Maribeth's father had been at Iwo Jima. Her mother had worried the whole time he was gone, but eventually he had come home safely.

"What would you do if you were drafted to go to war?" she asked, and he looked confused by the question.

"Now, you mean? Or when I'm eighteen?" It

was a possibility, and only two years away for him, if the police action in Korea wasn't settled.

"Whenever. Would you go?"

"Of course. I'd have to."

"I wouldn't, if I were a man. I don't believe in war," she said firmly, while he smiled. Sometimes she was funny. She had such definite ideas, and some of them were pretty crazy.

"That's because you're a girl. Men don't have a choice."

"Maybe they should. Or maybe they will one day. Quakers don't go to war. I think they're smarter than everyone."

"Maybe they're just scared," he said, accepting all the traditions he'd ever known, but Maribeth was not willing to accept them. She didn't accept many things, unless she truly believed them.

"I don't think they're scared. I think they're true to themselves and what they believe. I'd refuse to go to war if I were a man," Maribeth said stubbornly. "War is stupid."

"No, you wouldn't," Tommy grinned. "You'd fight, like everyone else. You'd have to."

"Maybe one day men won't just do what they 'have to.' Maybe they'll question it, and not just do what they're told to."

"I doubt that. And if they did, it would be chaos. Why should some men go and not others? What would they do? Run away? Hide somewhere? It's impossible, Maribeth. Leave wars to guys. They know what they're doing."

"That's the trouble. I don't think they do. They just get us into new wars every time they get bored. Look at this one. We just got out of the last one, and we're back in the soup again," she said disapprovingly, and he laughed.

"Maybe you should run for president," he teased, but he respected her ideas, and her willingness to be adventuresome in her thinking. There was something very courageous about her.

They decided to go for a walk around the lake then, and on the way back, he asked her if she wanted to go swimming. But she declined again, and he was curious why she never wanted to join him. There was a raft far out in the lake, and he wanted her to swim to it with him, but she just didn't want to do it.

"Come on, tell the truth," he said finally, "are you afraid of the water? It's no shame if you are. Just say it."

"I'm not. I just don't want to swim." She was a good swimmer, but there was no way she was going to take her father's shirt off.

"Then come on in." It was blazing hot, and she would have liked a cool dip with him, but she knew she couldn't. She was fully four and a half months pregnant. "Just walk into the water with me. It feels great." She agreed to do that, but go no farther. And the lake was shallow for a long time, so they were fairly far out when it began to drop off sharply. She stopped on a sandy ledge, and he swam out past her toward the raft and then back again, with long, smooth strokes. He had long, powerful arms and legs, and he was a great swimmer. He was back in minutes, and stood up beside her, where she waited.

"You're a great swimmer," she said admiringly.

"I was on the team at school last year, but the captain was a jerk. I'm not going to swim with the team this year." He was eyeing her with mischievous interest as they started to walk back toward shore and he splashed her. "You're a real chicken, you know. You probably swim as well as I do."

"No, I don't," she said, trying to duck his splashes. But he was playful with her, and she couldn't resist splashing him, and a moment later, they were like two children, throwing armfuls of water at each other. She was soaking wet, and she lost her footing as she ducked him, and sat down hard in the water. She looked surprised at first, and then she realized she was soaking wet, and there would be no way of getting out of the water without his seeing her protruding stomach. It was too late to salvage the situation, and so she tripped him, and he wound up in the water next to her, and then she swam away from him speedily, but he caught up to her with ease, and they were both spluttering and laughing.

She didn't swim out to the raft with him, but they swam together for a while, as she tried to figure out how to get out of the water gracefully, without having him see her stomach, but she just couldn't figure out how to do it. And then, finally, she told him she was cold, which she wasn't, and asked if he'd go and get her towel. He looked a little surprised, in the warm water and the heat of the afternoon sun, but he went to get it, and held it out to her. But she still had to get out of the water and walk toward him. She wanted to tell him to turn around, but she didn't dare, she just lay in the water looking worried.

"Is something wrong?" She didn't know what to say to him, and finally, reluctantly, she nodded. She hadn't wanted to tell him yet, and didn't know what she would say to him when she did. But she was trapped now. "Can I help?" He looked baffled.

"Not really."

"Look, just come out, Maribeth. Whatever it is, we'll work it out. Come on, I'll help you." He held a hand out to her, and the gesture brought tears to her eyes, and then he walked through the water toward her, and gently lifted her up, until she stood in front of him. She let him pull her clear of the water, and she didn't resist him as tears filled her eyes, and he had no idea why she was crying. He put the towel gently around her, and then as he looked down, he saw it, it was an undeniable bulge, still small, but very firm and very round, and very obviously a baby. He still remembered how his own mother had looked when she was expecting Annie, and

141

Maribeth was too thin for it to be anything else, and he looked back at her again in amazement.

"I didn't want you to know," she said miserably. "I didn't want to tell you." They were standing up to their knees in the lake, and neither of them moved toward shore as they stood there. He looked as though he had been struck by lightning, and she looked as though someone had died.

"Come on," he said quietly, pulling her closer to him and putting an arm around her shoulders, "let's go sit down." They walked silently back to the beach and the place where they had spread out their blanket. She took off the towel and then unbuttoned her father's shirt. She had a bathing suit and shorts under it, there was no point wearing it all now. Her secret was out in the open. "How did that happen?" he said finally, trying not to stare at the very obvious bulge as she sat there, but still amazed by it, and she smiled ruefully at his question.

"The usual way, I guess, not that I know much about it."

"You had a boyfriend? You *have* a boyfriend?" he corrected, as he felt his heart squeeze, but she shook her head and looked away and then back at him again.

"Neither one. I did something really stupid." She decided to make a clean breast of it with him. She wanted no secrets from him. "I did it once. With someone I hardly knew. I wasn't even out on a date with him. He took me home from a dance where my date got drunk, and he was kind of the senior hero. I guess I was flattered he'd even talk to me, and he was a lot smoother than I bargained for. He made a big fuss over me, and took me out for a hamburger with his friends, and I thought it was great, and then he stopped somewhere to park on the way home. I didn't want to go, but I didn't want to make a big deal about it either, and he gave me a sip of gin, and then . . ." she looked down at her protruding belly ". . . you can figure out the rest. He said he didn't think I could get pregnant. He'd broken up with his girlfriend that weekend, or so he said, and on Monday he went back to her, and I had made a total fool of myself. Better than that, I'd destroyed my life for a guy I didn't even know, and who would never care about me. It took me a while to figure out what had happened, and by the time I did, he was engaged. They got married right after graduation."

"Did you tell him?"

"Yeah, I did. He said he wanted to marry her, and she'd be really pissed if she knew . . . I didn't want to ruin his life . . . or my own. I wouldn't tell my parents who he was, because I didn't want my father forcing him to marry me. I don't want to be married to someone who doesn't love me. I'm sixteen. My life would be over. But on the other hand," she sighed as she sat, looking despondent, "my life may be over anyway. This hasn't exactly been a brilliant move on my part."

"What did your parents say?" He was over-whelmed by what she was telling him, the insensitivity of the guy, and her courage at not doing what she didn't want to, in the face of disaster.

"My father said I had to move out. He took me to the Sisters of Charity, and I was supposed to live with them until I had it. But I just couldn't do it. I stayed for a few weeks, and it was so depressing, I figured I'd rather starve, so I left and got on a bus, and came here. I bought a ticket to Chicago, and figured I'd try to get a job there, but we stopped here for dinner and I saw the sign in Jimmy's window. They gave me the job, and I got off the bus, and here I am." She looked vulnerable and incredibly young, and very beautiful as he watched her, overcome with tenderness and admiration. "My dad says I can come home after Christmas, *after* I have the baby. I'll go back to school then," she said weakly, trying to make it sound okay, but even to her own ears, it sounded dismal.

"What are you going to do with the baby?" he asked, still amazed at what had happened to her.

"Give it away . . . put it up for adoption. I want to find good people to take it. I can't take care of it. I'm sixteen. I can't take care of a baby . . . I have nothing to give it . . . I don't know what to do for it. I want to go back to school . . . I want to go to college . . . if I keep the

144

baby, I'll be stuck forever . . . and more than that, I'd have nothing to give it. I want to find a family that really wants it. The nuns said they'd help me, but that was back home . . . I haven't done anything about it here." She looked nervous as she talked to him about it, and he was stunned by all that she was saying.

"Are you sure you don't want to keep it?" He couldn't imagine giving a baby away. Even to him, it sounded awful.

"I don't know." She could feel the baby moving as she said it, as though it were fighting for some small voice in the decision. "I just don't see how I could take care of it. My parents wouldn't help me. I can't make enough money to support it . . . it wouldn't be fair to the baby. And I don't want a baby now. Is that really awful?" Her eyes filled with tears and she looked at him in despair. It was terrible admitting she didn't want this baby, but she didn't. She didn't love Paul, and she didn't want to have a child, or be responsible for someone else's life. She could hardly manage her own, let alone someone else's. She was only sixteen.

"Wow, Maribeth. You've got your hands full." He moved closer to her, and put an arm around her again, and pulled her close to him. "Why didn't you say anything? You could have told me."

"Oh yeah, sure . . . hi, my name is Maribeth, I'm knocked up by a guy who married someone else, and my parents threw me out . . . how about taking me to dinner?" He laughed at what she said, and she smiled through her tears, and then suddenly she was in his arms and crying with terror and shame, and relief that she had told him. The sobs that racked her drained her of all energy, and he held her until she stopped. He felt desperately sorry for her, and the baby.

"When's it due?" he asked when she had calmed down again.

"Not till the end of December." But that was only four months away, and they both knew it would come very quickly.

"Have you seen a doctor here?"

"I don't know anyone." She shook her head. "I didn't want to tell the girls at the restaurant, because I was afraid Jimmy would fire me. I told them I was married to a guy who was killed in Korea, so they wouldn't be too surprised when they finally saw I was pregnant."

"That was pretty good thinking," he said with a look of amusement, and then he looked at her questioningly again. "Were you in love with him, Maribeth? The father, I mean."

It meant a lot to Tommy to know if she had loved him. But he was relieved when she shook her head. "I was flattered he wanted to go out with me. That's all. I was just incredibly stupid. To tell you the truth, he's a jerk. He just wanted me to get lost and not tell Debbie. He told me I could get rid of it. I'm not even sure what they do, but I think they cut the baby out. Nobody would really tell me, and everyone says it's really dangerous and expensive."

Tommy looked at her soberly as she explained it to him. He had heard of abortions too, but he was no clearer than she was on the exact nature of the procedure. "I'm glad you didn't do it."

"Why?" His comment surprised her. What difference did it make to him? Things would have been so much simpler for them if she weren't pregnant.

"Because I don't think you should. Maybe this is one of those things, like Annie . . . maybe it happened for a reason."

"I don't know. I've thought about it a lot. I've tried to understand why this happened. But I don't. It just seems like such rotten luck. One time. I guess that's all it takes." He nodded tentatively. His knowledge of sex was as sketchy as hers was, possibly more so. And unlike Maribeth, he had never done it.

He looked at her very oddly then, and she could see he was dying to ask her another question.

"What? Go on . . . whatever it is . . . ask me . . ." They were friends to the death now, bound in a friendship that they both knew would last forever. He was part of her secret pact. He was part of it now. And he would always be part of it from this moment.

"What was it like?" he asked, looking red-faced and mortally embarrassed, but the question didn't horrify her. Nothing did now. He was like a brother, or a best friend, or something more than that. "Was it terrific?"

"No. Not for me. Maybe for him. But I think it could be . . . it was kind of exciting, and dizzy making. It makes you stop thinking of anything else, or making sense, or wanting to do the right thing. It's kind of like an express train once it gets under way, or maybe that was the gin . . . but I think with the right person, it might be pretty great. I don't know. I don't really want to try again. Not for a long time, and not till I find the right person. I don't want to do that again, and be really stupid." He nodded, intrigued by what she said. It was kind of what he had expected, and he admired her resolve. But he was sorry she had had the experience, and he hadn't. "The sad thing was that it didn't mean anything, and it should. And now I have this baby, whom nobody wants, not the father, not me, no one."

"Maybe you'll change your mind when you see it," he said thoughtfully. His heart had melted from the first moment he'd seen Annie.

"I'm not sure I will. The two girls who had babies at the convent before I left never saw their babies. The nuns just took them away when they were born, and that was it. It seems so strange to carry it with you all this time, and then give it away . . . but it seems just as strange to keep it. It's not like it's for one day. It's forever. Could I do that? Could I be a mother for all that time? I don't think so. And then I think that there's something wrong with me. Why don't I want this baby with me forever? And if I do when I see it, then what am I going to do? How will I support it, or keep it? Tommy, I don't know what to do. . . ." Her eyes filled with tears again and he pulled her close to him again, and this time, without hesitating, he leaned down and kissed her. It was a kiss filled with admiration and tenderness and compassion, and all the love he had come to feel for her. It was the kiss of a man for a woman, the first either had known in just that way, the first either had felt of that magnitude in their entire lifetime. It was a kiss that could easily lead to more, except that now, and here, neither of them would let it.

"I love you," he whispered into her hair afterwards, wishing that it was his baby she was carrying, and not that of a boy she had never cared for. "I love you so much . . . I won't go away . . . I'll be there to help you." They were brave promises for a sixteen-year-old boy. But in the past year he had grown into manhood.

"I love you too," she said cautiously, wiping away her tears with his towel, and not wanting to give him all her problems.

"You've got to go to a doctor," he said, sounding remarkably paternal.

"Why?" Sometimes she still seemed very young, in spite of what she was going through.

"You've got to make sure the baby's healthy. My mom went all the time when she was pregnant with Annie."

"Yeah, but she was older."

"I think you're supposed to go anyway." And then he had a thought. "I'll get the name of my mom's doctor, and maybe we can figure out a way for him to see you." He looked pleased with the idea, and she giggled.

"You're crazy. They'll think it's yours, and they'll tell your mom. I can't go to a doctor, Tommy."

"We'll figure something out," he tried to reassure her. "And maybe my mom's doctor could help you find someone to adopt it. I think they do that too. They must know people who want babies and can't have them. I think my mom and dad thought about adopting for a while, before they had Annie, and then they didn't have to. I'll get his name, and we can make an appointment." He had stepped right into it, and shouldered the burden with her, unlike anyone else in her life. He kissed her again long and hard, and then ever so gently, he put a hand on the baby. It was moving a lot then, and she asked him if he could feel it. He concentrated for a little while, and then with a grin, he nodded. It was just the tiniest of flutterings, as if her belly had a life of its own, which it did at the moment.

They went swimming again late that afternoon, and this time she swam to the raft with him, and she was tired when she got back. They lay on their blanket then for a long time, and talked quietly about her future. It seemed a little less ominous now, with Tommy to share it, although the enormity of it still scared her. If she kept it, she would have the child for the rest of her life. If not, she might always regret it. It was hard to know which was the right thing to do, except that she kept feeling that it would be a greater gift to the child, and even herself, to let it go to other parents. There would be other children one day, and she would always regret this one, but it was the wrong time and the wrong place, and circumstances she just couldn't manage.

He held her in his arms, and they kissed and snuggled but it went no further. They were both strangely peaceful when they went back to her room so she could change her clothes, to go out for dinner and a movie. Things had changed between them that afternoon. It was as though they belonged to each other now. She had shared her secret with him, and he had been there for her. She knew he wouldn't let her down. They needed each other, and she needed him especially. It was as though a silent bond had formed between them, a bond that would never be severed.

"See you tomorrow," he said when he dropped her off at her place at eleven o'clock. He knew he couldn't stay away from her now. He needed to know that she was all right. He was going to drive her home from work the next day, although he had promised his mother he'd be home for dinner. "Take care of yourself,

Maribeth," he smiled, and she smiled back at him with a wave, as she closed the door softly behind her. And as she got into bed, she thought about how lucky she had been to ever meet him. He was the kind of friend she had never had, the brother Ryan had never been, the lover Paul never could have been. For the moment, he was everything. And that night, once again, she dreamt of Annie.

Chapter Six

For the next week, Tommy came by the restaurant every afternoon. He drove her home at night, and on Sunday night, he took her out to dinner and a movie. But on her next day off, he refused to take her to the lake again. Instead, he had a plan for something a great deal more important. He had stealthily borrowed his mother's address and telephone book, and carefully written down the name and address of her doctor. After old Dr. Thompson had died, Avery MacLean had been Liz's obstetrician for years, and had delivered both her children. He was a white-haired gentleman of distinguished years, but his ideas and techniques were considerably more modern than his manners. He was courtly, and formal in some ways, but he was extremely up to date in all the modern practices, and Tommy knew how much his mother liked him. And he also knew that Maribeth had to see a doctor.

He had made the appointment in the name of Mrs. Robertson, and tried his best to sound like his father on the phone, deepening his voice and trying to sound confident, despite trembling fingers. He had claimed to be Mr. Robertson when they'd asked, and said that they had just moved to Grinnell, after getting married, and his wife needed a checkup. And the nurse sounded as though she believed him.

"But what'll I say to him?" Maribeth looked at him in panic when he told her.

"Won't he know just by examining you? Do you have to tell him?" Tommy tried to sound more confident then he felt, and more knowledgeable than he was. He was still pretty sketchy on most of the fine points of her problem. All he knew of pregnancy was what he had seen of his mother in voluminous clothes, six years before, and could still remember, and what he'd seen of *I Love Lucy* on TV the year before, when she announced that she was expecting.

"I mean . . . what'll I tell him about . . . about the baby's father . . ." She looked deeply worried, but she knew too that he was right. There was so much about her condition that she didn't know, and she needed to talk to a doctor.

"Just tell him what you told them at the restaurant, that he was killed in Korea." They didn't know about the baby yet, but she had laid the groundwork with her story about being a widow.

And then she looked up at him with eyes full of tears, and stunned him with her next question. "Will you come with me?"

"Me? I . . . what . . . what if they recognize me?" He was blushing to the roots of his hair at the mere thought of it. What if they examined her in front of him, what if they expected him to know something he didn't? He had no idea what mysteries transpired in the offices of women's doctors. Worse yet, what if they told his parents? "I can't, Maribeth . . . I just couldn't . . ."

She nodded, without saying a word, as one lone tear rolled slowly down her cheek, and he felt his heart rip right out of his body. "Okay . . . okay . . . don't cry . . . I'll think of something . . . maybe I could just say you're my cousin . . . but then he'd be sure to tell my mom . . . I don't know, Maribeth, maybe we can just say we're friends, and I knew your husband, and I just drove you over."

"Do you think he'll suspect anything? That I'm not married, I mean?" They were like two kids trying to figure out how to get themselves out of a mess they had unwittingly created. But it was a very big mess, and there was no getting out of this one.

"He won't know if you don't tell him anything," Tommy said firmly, trying to show a calm he didn't feel. He was terrified of going to the doctor with her. But he didn't want to let her down, and once he had told her he would, he knew he had to.

They were both nervous wrecks on their way to the appointment that afternoon. They barely spoke, and he felt so sorry for her, he tried to reassure her as he helped her out of the truck, and followed her into the doctor's office, praying that he wasn't blushing.

"It'll be okay, Maribeth . . . I promise." He whispered as they stepped inside, and she only nodded. Tommy had only met the man once outside the hospital where he had stood and waved with his dad after Annie was born. He was too young to go upstairs, and his mother had stood at the window of her room, waving at him, and proudly holding little Annie. Just thinking of it now brought tears to his eyes, and he squeezed Maribeth's hand, as much to encourage her as to comfort himself, as the head nurse looked up at them, over the rims of her glasses.

"Yes?" She couldn't imagine what they were doing there, except perhaps meeting their mother. They were both barely more than children. "May I help you?"

"I'm Maribeth Robertson . . ." she whispered, as her voice trailed off inaudibly on her last name, unable to believe that Tommy had actually made her come here. "I have an appointment with the doctor." The nurse frowned, looked down at her appointment book and then nodded.

"Mrs. Robertson?" She seemed surprised. Maybe the girl was a little older than she seemed. More than anything, she seemed extremely nervous.

"Yes." It was barely more than a sigh on her lips, as the nurse told them to take a seat in the waiting room and smiled to herself, remembering his call. They were obviously newlyweds, and barely more than kids themselves. She couldn't help wondering if they had had to get married.

156

They sat in the waiting room, whispering, and trying not to look at some of the enormously pregnant women around them. Tommy had never seen so many of them in one room, and it was profoundly embarrassing, as they chatted about their husbands, their other kids, patted their tummies from time to time, and knitted. And it was a merciful relief for both of them when Dr. MacLean called them both into his office. He referred to them as Mr. and Mrs. Robertson, and Tommy found himself feeling paralyzed when he didn't correct him. But the doctor had no reason to suspect that he was anything but Maribeth's husband. He asked them where they lived, where they were both from, and then finally how long they'd been married. And Maribeth looked at the doctor for a long moment and then shook her head.

"We're not . . . I am . . . that is . . . Tommy is just a friend . . . my husband died in Korea," and then, regretting the lie the moment it was said, she looked at him honestly, with tears in her eyes. "I'm not married, Doctor. I'm five months pregnant . . . and Tommy thought I should come to see you." He admired her for protecting the boy, and thought it unusually noble.

"I see." He looked sobered by everything she had said to him, and looked at Tommy for a long moment, thinking that he looked vaguely familiar. He wondered if he was the son of one of his patients. He knew he had seen him some-

157

where. In fact, he had gone to Annie's funeral and seen him there, but at the moment he couldn't remember where he'd seen him.

"And are you planning to get married soon?" He looked at both of them, sorry for them. He was always sorry for kids in their situation. But they both shook their heads, looking chagrined, as though they were afraid he was going to throw them both out of his office, and suddenly Tommy was sorry he had ever suggested that she go there.

"We're just friends," Maribeth said firmly. "This wasn't Tommy's fault. It was all mine." She had started to cry, and Tommy reached out and touched her hand as the doctor watched them.

"I think that's beside the point now," he said kindly. "Why don't you and I have a little chat alone for a while, and then we'll take a look at you, and your . . . friend," he smiled at the word, amused that they would think he wouldn't know what had happened, "your friend can come back and talk to us after that. How does that sound?" He wanted to examine her, and talk to her about what was happening, how her parents had reacted to her pregnancy, what her real plans were, and if she was going to keep the baby. They seemed very much in love to him, and he imagined they'd get married eventually, particularly since they'd come this far together. But their families were probably giving them a hard time, and he wanted to help them as much as he could. Maybe all they needed was a push in the right direction.

The doctor stood up then, and escorted Tommy from the room. And it was even more terrifying this time, sitting in a waiting room filled with pregnant women, without her. He just prayed that no one his mother knew would walk in and see him.

It seemed hours before the nurse beckoned to him, and led him back to the doctor's office.

"I thought you might like to come in with your friend and talk about things now," the doctor said warmly as he walked in. Maribeth was smiling at him, and she looked shy, but relieved. The doctor had listened to the baby's heart, and said it looked like it was going to be a big, healthy baby. She had told him too that she was probably going to be putting it up for adoption, and if he knew of anyone who would be right for it, she'd like to know about it. He had promised to think, but had said no more than that. And he seemed far more interested in sharing most of the information he'd told her with Tommy, about the baby's size and health, about what Maribeth could expect over the next few months, the vitamins she'd have to take, the naps she should take if her work schedule allowed. He told them all of it, as though Tommy were the baby's father, and then Tommy realized what was happening. Dr. MacLean thought that they were hiding from him the fact that Tommy was the father. And no matter how much Maribeth had insisted they were just friends, it was obvious that he didn't believe them. It was much too obvious to him how much Tommy cared about her, and how much he loved her.

And as he looked at them both, and explained about his fees, something stirred in his memory, and suddenly he realized who the boy was, and he was pleased that he had brought Maribeth to him.

"You're Tommy Whittaker, aren't you, son?" he asked gently. He didn't want to frighten him, he was willing to share their secret with them, as long as neither of them got hurt by it, and he didn't have a compelling reason to tell his parents.

"Yes, I am," Tommy said honestly.

"Do your parents know about this?"

Tommy shook his head, blushing terribly. It was impossible to explain that he had stolen his mother's address book to get the number. "They haven't met Maribeth." He would have liked to introduce her to them, but he couldn't under the circumstances, and things were just too difficult with his parents now anyway.

"Maybe it's time you introduced them," Dr. MacLean said wisely. "You can't wait forever. Christmas will be here before you know it." It was only four months until her due date. "Think about it, your parents are pretty understanding people. They've been through an awful lot recently, and I'm sure this would come as a shock

160

to them, but at least they could help you." Maribeth had told him that she was estranged from her family, and the only friend she had in the world was Tommy. "This is a mighty big burden for you to be carrying alone on those young shoulders."

"We're okay," he said bravely, compounding the problem, and convincing the doctor again that the baby was his, no matter how much Maribeth denied it. It was sweet the way she protected him from any blame, and it impressed the doctor about her. He was impressed by both of them, and glad they had come to him. And he made another appointment for her the following month, and handed them a very simple book before they left, explaining to them what to expect over the next four months, and at the delivery. There were no photographs, just a few simple drawings, and neither of them had ever seen a book like it. It assumed a certain amount of knowledge that neither of them had, and many of the terms used were completely unfamiliar. But it also told Maribeth how to take care of herself, what to do, and what not to do, and danger signals along the way that would warrant calling the doctor. They both thought it was pretty impressive.

Dr. MacLean had told Maribeth he would charge two hundred and fifty dollars for all her prenatal care, and to deliver her, and the hospital charges would be another three hundred, which fortunately she still had set aside from the money her father had originally given her for the convent. So she had enough to pay for it. But they were both more than a little concerned that he thought Tommy was the baby's father.

"What if he tells your mom?" she asked, terrified. She didn't want to create a problem for him. And Tommy was worried too, but he had somehow gotten the impression that the doctor wouldn't betray them. He was a decent man, and he just didn't think Dr. MacLean would tell his parents. And despite the misunderstanding over who the baby's father was, he was glad he had taken Maribeth to see him.

"I don't think he will," he reassured her. "I really think he wants to help us." Tommy trusted him and he felt certain he was right to do so.

"He's nice," she said, and then they went out for milkshakes. They talked in whispers about the book he'd given her, about the trimester she was in, and some of the things the doctor had said about labor and delivery. "It sounds pretty scary," Maribeth said nervously. "He said he could give me some stuff to make me sleepy . . . I think I'd like that." She wasn't sure about the whole thing. It was a lot to go through at sixteen, for a baby she wouldn't keep and would never see again. It was a lot to ask, for half an hour in the front seat of a Chevy with Paul Browne. Sometimes she still couldn't believe it was happening. But seeing the doctor made it more real. As did Tommy's concern, and the fact that suddenly the baby seemed to be growing daily.

Tommy came to see her at the restaurant almost every day, or else he showed up at her house after work and took her out for a soda, or a walk, or a movie. But on the first of September, he went back to school, and after that everything was harder. He had classes till three in the afternoon, and then sports, and his paper route. By the time he got to see her in the early evening, he was exhausted. But he was always concerned about her, and whenever they were alone, he held her in his arms and kissed her. And sometimes it felt as though they were already married, as they chatted about the day, her job, his school, and their problems. The passion between them felt married too, except that neither of them ever let it go further than it should. It never went beyond kissing and holding and touching.

"I don't want to get pregnant," she said hoarsely one night, as his hands wandered over her slowly swelling breasts, and they both laughed. She didn't want to make love with him, not now, with Paul's baby in her . . . and afterwards, she wanted it to be different. She didn't want this to happen again, until she wanted it to, long years from now, after she went back to school, and college, and married the right man, then she'd want his babies. She didn't want to do it with Tommy too soon, and spoil everything, but he understood that, although it drove him crazy sometimes because he wanted her so badly.

Sometimes he did his homework at her place,

or at the restaurant, in a back corner, while she brought him milkshakes and hamburgers, and sometimes she even helped him. And when her landlady was out, and her door was locked they stretched out on her bed sometimes, and he read to her, or she did his chemistry for him, or his algebra or trig. They were an even match academically, and it was two weeks after school had begun for him that it suddenly dawned on him that they could do all the work together. He was going to copy the curriculum for her, and lend her his books, and that way she could stay abreast of the work she was missing in her own school, and continue her education.

"You can ask them to take an exam when you go back, and you won't have to miss the semester." But that was something he didn't like to think about, her going back to Iowa and her parents. He wanted her to stay with him, but neither of them knew yet exactly what would happen after she had the baby.

But for the moment, his plan was working extremely well. They met every night after school, and work when she could, and both of them did the homework. She kept the papers she did, and she did all the same assignments. In effect, she was continuing school, and working at Jimmy's too, and Tommy was very impressed with the quality of the schoolwork she was doing. And in spite of his good grades, he realized within days that she was actually an even stronger student than he was.

"You're good," Tommy said admiringly, correcting some algebra for her, from the sheet they'd given him at school. She'd had an A+ on both quizzes he'd passed on to her that week, and he thought her history paper about the Civil War was the best he'd ever read. He wished his history teacher could see it.

The only problem for them was that he was getting home at midnight every night, and by the end of the first month of school, his mother was getting suspicious. He explained to her that he had sports practice every day, and was tutoring a friend who was having a lot of trouble with math, but with his mother working at the school, it wasn't easy convincing her that he was justified in coming home at midnight.

But he loved being with Maribeth. They talked for hours sometimes after they finished their work, about their dreams and ideals, the issues their assignments brought out about values and goals and ethics, and inevitably they talked about the baby, about what she hoped for it, the kind of life she wanted it to have. She wanted it to have so much more than she had. She wanted it to have the best education it could get, and parents who wanted to help it move ahead into the world, not back into positions forged by the fears or ignorance of past generations. Maribeth knew what kind of fight she herself was going to have trying to get to college one day. Her parents thought it was frivolous and unnecessary, and they would never understand it. But she didn't want to be confined to a job like the one she had now. She knew she could do so much more with her life, if she could just get an education.

Her teachers had always tried to tell her parents that she could go far, but they just didn't understand it. And now her father would say that she was just like her aunts, and had managed to get herself knocked up out of wedlock. She knew she would never live that down, and even without the baby in her arms, they would never let her forget it.

"Then why don't you keep it?" Tommy said to her more than once, but she would shake her head at that. She knew that that wasn't the answer either. No matter how far along she got, or how sweet the feelings were, she knew she couldn't take care of it, and in some part of herself, she knew she didn't want to.

By early October, she had to admit to the girls at work that she was pregnant. They had figured it out for themselves by then too, and they were excited for her, imagining that it was a last gift from her dead husband, a wonderful way of holding on to his memory forever. They had no way of knowing that it was Paul Browne's memory, someone whose eighteen-year-old wife was probably already pregnant by then too, and didn't care about this baby.

She couldn't tell them that she wanted to give the baby up, and they brought small gifts in to work for her, which always made her feel terribly guilty. She set them aside in a drawer in her room, and tried not to think about the baby that would wear them.

She also went to see Dr. MacLean again, and he was very pleased with her, and always asked about Tommy.

"Such a fine boy," he smiled, talking to her, sure that their mistake would have a happy outcome. They were both nice kids. She was a lovely girl, and he was sure that the Whittakers would adjust to it, and accept her once they knew about the baby. And it was mid-October when by sheer coincidence Liz Whittaker came in from school one day for her checkup. And then, before she left, he remembered to tell her what a fine boy her son was.

"Tommy?" She looked startled that he remembered him. The last time he had seen the boy was six years before when Annie was born, and he had stood outside the hospital and waved up at her window. "He is a good boy," she agreed, sounding puzzled.

"You should be very proud," he said knowingly, wanting to say more about the two young people who had impressed him so much, but he knew he couldn't. He had promised both of them he wouldn't.

"I am proud of him," she said, distracted by her rush to get back to school, but on her way home later she thought about his comment again, and wondered if he'd run into Tommy somewhere. Maybe he had taught a class at school, or had a child in Tommy's class, and then she forgot about it.

But the following week, one of her colleagues said they had seen Tommy with a remarkably pretty girl, and casually mentioned that the girl looked extremely pregnant.

She was horrified when she heard about it, and then with a rush of terror, remembered Dr. MacLean's unexpected praise of Tommy. She thought about it all afternoon, and then decided to ask Tommy about it that night. But he didn't even come home until after midnight.

"Where have you been?" his mother asked in stern tones when he got in. She had been waiting up for him in the kitchen.

"Studying with some friends," he answered, looking nervous.

"What friends?" She knew almost all of them, particularly now that she was teaching at the high school. "Who? I want to know their names."

"Why?" Tommy suddenly looked very guarded, and when his father came into the room, he saw an odd look pass between his parents. The hostility between them had lessened a little bit since his mother had gone back to work, but the distance seemed greater than ever. Liz had said nothing to John about the girl someone had seen Tommy with, but he had heard them talking, and wondered what was going on. Lately, he had been increasingly aware of the fact that Tommy was literally never home, and

168

coming home very late in the evening.

"What's up?" he asked Liz, not really looking worried. Tommy was a good boy, and he had never gotten into trouble. Maybe he had a girl-friend.

"I've been hearing some strange things about Tommy," his mother said, looking concerned, "and I want to hear from him about it." But as he looked at her, Tommy knew that she knew something.

"What kind of 'strange' things?" John asked. It didn't sound like Tommy.

"Who's the girl you've been seeing?" his mother asked him bluntly, as his father sat down and watched them.

"Just a friend. No one special." But it was a lie, and she sensed that. Maribeth was more than a friend to him. He was head over heels in love with her, trying to help her keep up with school, and deeply concerned about her baby.

But his mother didn't pull any punches. "Is she pregnant?" He looked as though she had lev-eled a blow to his diaphragm and his father looked as though he was going to fall out of his chair, as Liz stared at Tommy in the silence. "Well, is she?"

"I . . . no . . . I . . . gee, Mom . . . I don't know . . . I didn't . . . well . . . oh God . . . ," he agonized as he ran a hand through his hair and looked panicked. "I can explain. It's not what it looks like."

"She's just fat?" his father asked hopefully,

and Tommy looked rueful.

"Not exactly."

"Oh my God," his mother whispered.

"You'd better sit down," John said to him, and Tommy sank into a chair, as Liz continued to stand and stare at him in horror.

"I can't believe this," she said, in anguished tones. "She's pregnant . . . Tommy, what have you been doing?"

"I haven't been doing anything. We're just friends. I . . . all right . . . we're more than that . . . but . . . oh Mom . . . you'd like her."

"Oh my God," his mother said again, and this time she sat down. "Who is she? And how did this happen?"

"The usual way, I guess," Tommy added, looking bleak. "Her name is Maribeth. I met her this summer."

"Why didn't you tell us?" But how could he tell them anything? They never talked to him anymore, or each other. Their family life had ended when Annie died, now they just drifted, like flotsam on a lonely ocean. "How pregnant is she?" his mother asked, as though that would make a difference.

"Six and a half months," he said calmly. Maybe it was better that they knew after all. He had wanted to ask his mother to help her for a long time, and he had always thought she would like her. But now Liz looked even more horrified.

"*Six and a half months?* When did this start?"

She tried desperately to count backwards, and was too upset to do it.

"When did what start?" Tommy looked confused. "I told you, I met her this summer. She only moved here in June. She works at a restaurant I go to."

"When do you go to a restaurant?" His father looked even more confused than his mother.

"Lots of times. Mom never cooks anymore. She hasn't in months. I use some of my paper money to pay for dinner."

"That's nice," his father said tartly, glaring at his wife reproachfully, and then at his son again, in confusion. "How old is this girl?"

"Sixteen."

"I don't understand," his mother interrupted. "She moved here in June, and she's six and a half months pregnant . . . that means she got pregnant in March, or somewhere around then. You got her pregnant somewhere else, and she moved here? Where were you?" He hadn't gone anywhere that they knew of. But they also didn't know that he frequently went out to dinner, nor that he had a pregnant girlfriend. Six and a half months made the baby imminent. Liz trembled as she thought of it. What were they thinking of, and why hadn't he told them? But as she thought about it, she began to understand. They had all been so distant and so lost since Annie died, particularly she and John, no wonder Tommy had gotten himself into trouble. No one had been paying attention.

171

But Tommy had finally understood the nature of their questions. "I didn't get her pregnant, Mom. She got pregnant back home, in Onawa, and her father made her leave until after the baby. She went to live in a convent and she couldn't stand it, so she came here in June. And that's when I met her."

"And you've been going out with her all this time? Why didn't you tell us?"

"I don't know," he sighed, "I wanted to, because I really thought you'd like her, but I was afraid you wouldn't approve. She's wonderful, and she's all alone. She doesn't have anyone to help her."

"Except you." His mother looked pained, but his father was relieved. "Which reminds me," Liz asked as she began to unravel the story, "have you been taking her to Dr. MacLean?"

Tommy looked startled by her question. "Why? Did he say anything?" He shouldn't have, he had promised he wouldn't, but his mother shook her head as she watched him.

"He didn't really say anything. He just said what a nice boy you were, and I couldn't figure out how he remembered. It's been six years . . . and then one of the teachers saw you with her last week, and said she looked extremely pregnant." She looked up at her sixteen-year-old son then, wondering if he intended to marry the girl, out of real emotion for her, or even just to be gallant. "What's she going to do with the baby?"

"She's not sure. She doesn't think she can take

care of it. She wants to put it up for adoption. She thinks it's kinder to do that, for the baby's sake. She has this theory," he wanted to explain it all to her at once, to make them love her as much as he did, "that some people pass through other people's lives just for a short time, like Annie, to bring a blessing or a gift of some kind . . . she feels that way about this baby, as though she's here to bring it into the world, but not to be in its life forever. She feels very strongly about it."

"That's a very big decision for a young girl to make," Liz said quietly, sorry for her, but worried about Tommy's obvious infatuation. "Where's her family?"

"They won't speak to her or let her come home until after she gives up the baby. Her father sounds like a real jerk, and her mother is scared of him. She's really on her own."

"Except for you," Liz said sadly. It was a terrible burden for him to bear, but John wasn't nearly as worried now that he knew it wasn't his baby.

"I'd like you to meet her, Mom." She hesitated for a long time, not sure if she wanted to dignify the relationship by meeting her, or simply forbid him to see her. But that didn't seem fair to him, and she glanced silently at her husband. John shrugged, showing that he had no objection.

"Maybe we should." In a funny way, she felt that they owed it to Tommy. If he thought so much of this girl, maybe she was worth meeting.

"She's desperate to go to school. I've been working with her every night, lending her my books, and giving her copies of everything we've done. She's way ahead of me by now, and she does a lot more papers and independent reading."

"Why isn't she in school?" his mother asked, looking disapproving.

"She has to work. She can't go back to school till she goes home, after the baby."

"And then what?" His mother was pressing him, and even Tommy didn't have all the answers. "What about you? Is this serious?"

He hesitated, not wanting to tell her everything, but he knew he had to. "Yeah, Mom . . . it's serious. I love her."

His father looked suddenly panicked at his answer. "You're not going to marry her, are you? Or keep the kid? Tommy, at sixteen, you don't know what you're doing. It would be bad enough if the baby was yours, but it isn't. You don't have to do that."

"I know I don't," he said, looking like a man as he answered his father. "I love her. I would marry her if she would, *and* keep the baby, but she doesn't want to do either one. She wants to go back to school, and college if she can. She thinks she can still live at home, but I'm not sure she can. I don't think her father will ever let her get an education, from the sound of it. But she doesn't want to marry anyone until she's gotten an education. She's not trying to pressure me, Dad. If I married her, I'd have to force her to do it."

"Well, don't," his father said, opening a beer, and taking a sip. The very idea of Tommy getting married at sixteen unnerved him.

"Don't do anything you'll regret later, Tommy," his mother said, trying to sound calmer than she felt. But after all she'd heard, her hands were shaking. "You're both very young. You'll ruin your lives if you make a mistake. She's already made one mistake, don't compound it with another."

"That's what Maribeth says. That's why she wants to give the baby up. She says keeping it would be just one more mistake that everyone would pay for. I think she's wrong, I think she'll be sorry one day that she gave it up, but she thinks it deserves a better life than she can give it."

"She's probably right," his mother said sadly, unable to believe that there was anything sadder in life than giving up a baby, except maybe losing one, especially a child you'd loved. But giving up a baby you'd carried for nine months sounded like a nightmare. "There are lots of wonderful people out there, anxious to adopt . . . people who can't have children of their own, and would be very good to a baby."

"I know." He looked suddenly very tired. It was one-thirty in the morning, and they had been sitting in the kitchen for an hour and a

175

half, discussing Maribeth's problem. "I just think it sounds so sad. And what will she have?"

"A future. Maybe that's more important," his mother said wisely. "She won't have a life, if she's dragging a baby around at sixteen, with no family to help her. And neither will you, if you marry her. That's not a life for two kids who haven't even finished high school."

"Just meet her, Mom. Talk to her. I want you to get to know her, and maybe you can give her some stuff from school. She's already gone way past me and I don't know what to give her."

"All right." His parents looked worried as they exchanged a glance, but they both nodded agreement. "Bring her home next week. I'll cook dinner." She made it sound like a major sacrifice. She hated cooking anymore, but she did it when she had to, and now she felt guiltier than ever about it, if it had driven her son to eating in restaurants, like an orphan. She tried to say something to him about that as they turned off the lights and walked down the hall. "I'm sorry I . . . I'm sorry I haven't been there very much for you," she said, as tears filled her eyes, and she stood on tiptoe to kiss him. "I love you . . . I guess I've been kind of lost myself for the past ten months."

"Don't worry about it, Mom," he said gently, "I'm fine." And he was now, thanks to Maribeth. She had helped him even more than he had helped her. They had brought each other a great deal of comfort.

Tommy went to his room, and in their own room Liz looked at John and sat down heavily on their bed, looking shattered.

"I can't believe what I just heard. You know, he'd marry the girl, if we let him."

"He'd be a damn fool if he did," John said angrily. "She's probably a little slut if she got herself pregnant at sixteen, and she's selling him a bill of goods about wanting an education, and college."

"I don't know what to think," Liz said, as she looked up at him, "except that I think we've all gone pretty crazy in the past year. You've been drinking, I've been gone, lost somewhere in my own head, trying to forget what happened. Tommy's been eating in restaurants and having an affair with a pregnant girl he wants to marry. I'd say we're a fair-sized mess, wouldn't you?" she asked, looking stunned by everything she'd just heard, and feeling very guilty.

"Maybe that's what happens to people when the bottom falls out of their lives," he said, sitting down on the bed next to her. It was the closest they'd been in a long time, and for the first time in a long time, Liz realized she didn't feel angry, just worried. "I thought I was going to die when . . ." John said softly, unable to finish his own sentence.

"So did I . . . I think I did," she admitted. "I feel like I've been in a coma for the past year. I'm not even sure what happened."

He put an arm around her then, and held her for a long time, and that night when they went to bed, he didn't say anything to her, or she to him, he just held her.

Chapter Seven

Tommy picked Maribeth up on her day off, and she had put on her best dress to go to his house and meet his parents. He had come to pick her up after football practice, and he was late, and he seemed more than a little nervous.

"You look really nice," he said, looking at her, and then he bent down and kissed her. "Thank you, Maribeth." He knew she really wanted to make an effort to meet his parents. She knew it was important to him, and she didn't want to embarrass him. It was bad enough that she was almost seven months pregnant. No one else in the world would have taken her to meet anyone, let alone their parents, except Tommy.

She was wearing a dark gray wool dress, with a little white collar and a black bow tie, that she had bought with her salary when she outgrew everything else she owned, and Tommy started taking her out for dinner on her days off from Jimmy's. And she had combed her bright red hair into a tight ponytail tied with a black velvet ribbon. She looked like a little kid hiding a big balloon under her skirt, and he smiled as he helped her into his dad's truck. She looked so cute, and she hoped that the meeting with his parents would go smoothly. They had said very little to him after their long talk the week before, except that they wanted to meet her. And Maribeth was excruciatingly quiet on the drive over.

"Don't be nervous, okay?" he said, as they stopped in front of his house, and she admired how tidy it looked. It was freshly painted and there were neat flower beds outside. There were no flowers there at this time of year, but it was easy to see that the house was well cared for. "It's going to be fine," he reassured her as he helped her down, and walked ahead of her into his house, holding her hand as he opened the door and saw his parents. They were waiting in the living room for them, and he saw his mother watch Maribeth as she quickly crossed the room to shake her hand, and then his father's.

Everyone was extremely circumspect and polite, and Liz invited her to sit down and then offered her tea or coffee. She had a Coke instead, and John chatted with her while Liz went to check on dinner. She had made pot roast for them, and the potato pancakes Tommy loved, with creamed spinach.

Maribeth offered to help after a little while, and she wandered into the kitchen to join Tommy's mother. The two men glanced down the hall after her, and John touched Tommy's arm to stop him when he seemed about to follow her into the kitchen.

"Let her talk to your mom, Son. Let your mother get to know her. She seems like a nice girl," he said fairly. "Pretty too. It's a shame this had to happen to her. What happened to the boy? Why didn't they get married?"

"He married someone else instead, and Maribeth didn't want to marry him, Dad. She said she didn't love him."

"I'm not sure if that's smart of her, or very foolish. Marriage can be difficult enough sometimes, without marrying someone you don't care about. But it was brave of her to do that." He lit his pipe and watched his son. Tommy had grown up a lot lately. "It doesn't seem fair that her parents won't see her until she has the baby," John said, looking at his son carefully, wondering how much this girl meant to him, and he could see that she meant a great deal. His heart was bare for all to see, and his father's heart went out to him.

When Liz called them to dinner finally, she and Maribeth seemed to have become friends. Maribeth was helping put things on the table, and they were talking about a senior civics class Liz was teaching. When Maribeth said she wished she could take something like it, Liz said thoughtfully, "I suppose I could give you some of the material. Tommy said you've been trying to keep up with your schoolwork, by doing his with him. Would you like me to look over some of your papers?" Maribeth looked stunned by the offer.

"I'd love that," she said gratefully, taking her place between the two men.

"Are you submitting anything to your old

school, or just doing it for yourself?"

"For myself mostly, but I was hoping they'd let me take some exams when I go back, to see if I could get credit for what I've been doing."

"Why don't you let me look at it, maybe I could submit it to our school for some kind of equivalency here. Have you done all of Tommy's work?" Maribeth was quick to nod in answer, and Tommy spoke up on her behalf as he sat down between Maribeth and his mother.

"She's gone a lot further than I have, Mom. She's already finished my science book for the whole year, and European history, and she's done all of the optional papers." Liz looked impressed and Maribeth promised to bring all her work by that weekend.

"I could give you some extra assignments actually," Liz said, as she handed the pot roast to Maribeth. "All of my classes are for juniors and seniors." They both looked excited as they continued to discuss it. And by the end of dinner, Liz and Maribeth had worked out an excellent plan to meet on Saturday afternoon for a few hours, and on Sunday Liz was going to give her half a dozen special assignments. "You can work on them whenever you can, and bring them back when you have the chance. Tommy says you work a six-day week at the restaurant, and I know that can't be easy." In fact Liz was surprised she still had the energy to work ten-hour shifts on her feet, waiting on tables. "How long will you be working, Maribeth?" She was embarrassed to ask about her pregnancy, but it was difficult to avoid it, her stomach was huge by then.

"Till the end, I think. I can't really afford not to." She needed the money her father had given her to pay for the delivery and Dr. MacLean, and she needed her salary to live on. She really couldn't afford to quit early. Just supporting herself after the baby for a week or two was going to be a challenge. Things were pretty tight for her, but fortunately she didn't need much. And since she wasn't keeping the baby, she hadn't bought anything for it, though the girls at the restaurant kept talking about giving her a shower. She tried to discourage them, because it just made it all the more poignant, but they had no idea she wasn't keeping her baby.

"That's going to be hard on you," Liz said sympathetically, "working right up until the end. I did that when Tommy was born, and I thought I'd have him right in the classroom. I took a lot more time before Annie," she said, and then there was sudden silence at the table. She looked up at Maribeth then, and the young girl met her eyes squarely. "I suppose Tommy has told you about his sister," she said softly.

Maribeth nodded, and her eyes were filled with her love for him, and her sympathy for his parents. Annie was so real to her, she had heard so many stories, and dreamt of her so many times that she almost felt as though she knew her. "Yes, he did," Maribeth said softly, "she

183

must have been a very special little girl."

"She was," Liz agreed, looking devastated, and then quietly, John reached his hand to her across the table. He just touched her fingers with his own, and Liz looked up in surprise. It was the first time he had ever done that. "I suppose all children are," she went on, "yours will be too. Children are a wonderful blessing." Maribeth didn't answer her, and Tommy glanced up at her, knowing the conflict she felt about the baby.

They talked about Tommy's next football game then, and Maribeth wished silently that she could join them.

They chatted for a long time, about Maribeth's hometown, her schooling, the time she had spent that summer at the lake with Tommy. They talked of many things, but not her relationship with their son, and not her baby. And at ten o'clock, Tommy finally drove her home, she kissed both his parents goodbye before she left, and once they were in the truck, she heaved a sigh of relief and lay back against the seat as though she was exhausted.

"How was I? Did they hate me?" He looked touched that she would even ask, and leaned over to kiss her ever so gently.

"You were wonderful, and they loved you. Why do you think my mother offered to help you with your work?" He was enormously relieved. His parents had been a lot more than polite, they were downright friendly. In fact, they

184

had been very impressed with her, and as John helped Liz do the dishes once they'd left, he complimented Maribeth on her bright mind and good manners.

"She's quite a girl, don't you think, Liz? It's such a damn shame she's gone and done this to herself." He shook his head and dried a dish. It was the first dinner he'd enjoyed as much in months, and he was pleased that Liz had made the effort.

"She didn't exactly do it to herself," Liz said with a small smile. But she had to admit he was right. She was a lovely girl, and she said as much to Tommy when he came back half an hour later. He had walked Maribeth to her room, he kissed her and could see that she was really tired and her back had been aching. It was a long day for her, and in the past couple of days she had begun to feel uncomfortable and awkward.

"I like your friend," Liz said quietly as she put the last dish away. John had just lit a pipe, and nodded as Tommy came in, to indicate his agreement.

"She liked you too. I think it's been really lonely for her, and she misses her parents and her little sister. They don't sound like much to me, but I guess she's used to them. Her father sounds like a real tyrant, and she says her mother never stands up to him, but I think it's really hard for her being cut off. Her mother has written to her a couple of times, but apparently her father won't even read her letters. And they won't let her communicate with her sister. Seems kind of dumb to me," he said, looking annoyed, and his mother watched his eyes. It was easy to see how much he loved her, and he was anxious to protect her.

"Families make foolish decisions sometimes," his mother said, feeling sorry for her. "I would think this will hurt them for a long time, maybe forever."

"She says she wants to go back and finish school, and then move to Chicago. She says she wants to go to college there."

"Why not here?" his father suggested, and Liz looked surprised at the ease with which he said it. It was a college town, and it was a very good school, if she could get a scholarship, and if she wanted to, Liz could help her with her application.

"I never thought of it, and I'm not sure she did either," Tommy said, looking pleased. "I'll talk to her about it, but I think right now, she's mostly worried about the baby. She's kind of scared. I don't think she knows what to expect. Maybe," he looked hesitantly at Liz, glad that the two women had met. "Maybe you could talk to her, Mom. She really doesn't have anyone else except me to talk to, and the other waitresses at Jimmy D's. And most of the time, I think they just scare her." From the little Tommy knew about what she'd be going through, it scared him too. The entire process sounded really awful.

"I'll talk to her," Liz said gently, and a little while later they all went to bed. And as Liz lay next to John, she found herself thinking about her. "She's a sweet girl, isn't she? I can't imagine going through all that alone . . . it would be so sad . . . and giving the baby up . . ." Just thinking about it brought tears to her eyes, as she remembered holding Annie for the first time, and Tommy . . . they had been so adorable and so warm and dear. The thought of giving them up at birth would have killed her. But she had waited for them for such a long time, and she was so much older. Maybe at sixteen it was all just too much, and Maribeth was wise to realize that it was more than she could cope with. "Do you suppose Avery will find a family for the child?" She was suddenly concerned about her. Like Tommy, she couldn't resist the fact that Maribeth had no one else to turn to.

"I'm sure he does it more often than we suspect. It's not uncommon, you know. It's just that usually girls in her situation are hidden away somewhere. I'm sure he'll find someone very suitable for her baby."

Liz nodded, as she lay in the dark, thinking about both of them, Maribeth and her son. They were so young and so much in love, and filled with hope. They still believed that life would be kind, and trusted in what their destinies would bring them. Liz no longer had that kind of faith, she had suffered too much pain when Annie died. She knew she would never trust the fates

187

again. They were too cruel, and too quixotic.

They talked about her for a while, and then John finally drifted off to sleep. In some ways, they were no closer than they had been, but these days the distance between them seemed less forbidding, and every now and then, there was some gesture or kind word that warmed her. She was making a little more effort for him, and dinner that night had really shown her that she needed to get back to cooking dinner. They needed to be together at night, needed to touch each other again, and listen and talk and bring each other hope again. They had all been lost for too long, and slowly Liz could feel them coming out of the mists where they had hidden. She could almost see John, reaching out to her, or wanting to, and Tommy was there, where he had always been, only now Maribeth was standing beside him.

She felt peaceful for the first time in months when she drifted off to sleep that night, and the next morning, at the school library, she began pulling books for Maribeth and writing down assignments. She was completely prepared for her when she came to visit that Saturday afternoon, and she was surprised by the quality of the work Maribeth handed her. She was doing higher quality work than most of the seniors.

Liz frowned as she read some of it, and shook her head. And Maribeth panicked as she watched her. "Is it bad, Mrs. Whittaker? I really didn't have much time to do it at night. I can do more work on it, and I want to do another book report on *Madame Bovary*. I don't think that one really does the book justice."

"Don't be ridiculous," Liz chided her, glancing up with an unexpected smile. "This is extraordinary. I'm very impressed." She made even Tommy's work seem weak by comparison, and he was a straight-A student. She had written a paper on Russian literature, and another on the humor of Shakespeare. She had done an editorial piece on the Korean war, as a writing assignment for English comp, and all of her math work was meticulous and perfect. It was all the highest quality work Liz had seen in years, and she looked up at the immensely pregnant girl and squeezed her hand gently. "You did a wonderful job, Maribeth. You should get a whole year's credit for this, or more. You've actually done senior-caliber work here."

"Do you really think so? Do you think I could submit it to my old school?"

"I have a better idea," Liz said, putting the folders in a neat pile. "I want to show these to our principal, maybe I can get you credit here. They might even let you take equivalency exams, and when you go home, you could go right in as a senior."

"Do you think they'd really let me do that?" Maribeth was stunned, and overwhelmed by what Liz was suggesting. It could mean jumping ahead a whole year, and maybe even finishing in June, which she really wanted. She knew that

189

even the next few months at home would be painful. She had proven to herself now that she could take care of herself, and she wanted to go home again, just to be there, and see her mother and Noelle and finish school. But she knew now that she wouldn't be able to stay for very long. She had come too far, and would have grown too much to stay at home for another two years after she gave up her baby. She knew they would never let her live it down, especially her father. Six months, until graduation in June, would be plenty. And then she could move on, get a job, and maybe one day, if she was lucky, get a scholarship to college. She was even willing to go at night. She was prepared to do anything for an education, and she knew her family would never understand that.

Liz gave her a number of additional assignments then, and promised to see what she could do at school, and she told Maribeth she'd let her know, as soon as they told her.

They talked for a while after that, about other things than school, mostly about Tommy, and his plans. Liz was obviously still worried that he would marry her, just so she wouldn't have to give up the baby, but Liz didn't say that. She just talked about the colleges she hoped he would attend, and the opportunities open to him, and Maribeth understood her completely. She knew what Liz was saying to her, and she couldn't help herself finally. She looked straight at her, and spoke very softly.

"I'm not going to marry him, Mrs. Whittaker. Not now anyway. I wouldn't do that to him. He's been wonderful to me. He's the only friend I've had since all this happened. But we're both too young, it would ruin everything. I'm not sure he really understands that," she said sadly, ". . . but I do. We're not ready for a child. At least I'm not. You have to give it so much, you have to be there for your kids . . . you have to be someone I'm not yet . . . you have to be grown up," she said with eyes filled with tears, as Liz's heart went out to her. She was barely more than a child herself, with a child of her own in her belly.

"You seem very grown up to me, Maribeth. Maybe not grown up enough to do all that . . . but you've got a lot to give. You do whatever is right for you . . . and for the baby. I just don't want Tommy to get hurt, or do something foolish."

"He won't," she said, smiling as she wiped her eyes, "I won't let him. Sure, sometimes I'd like to keep the baby too. But what then? What am I going to do, next month, or next year . . . or if I can't get a job, or there's no one to help me? And how is Tommy going to finish school, with a baby? He can't, and neither can I. I know it's my baby, and I shouldn't be talking like this, but I want what's right for the baby too. It has a right to so much more than I can give it. It has a right to parents who are crazy about it, and not scared to take care of it like I am. I

want to be there for it, but I know I just can't
. . . and that scares me." The thought of it tore
at her heart sometimes, especially now, with the
baby so big and so real, and moving all the time.
It was hard to ignore it, harder still to deny it.
But for her, loving her child meant giving it a
better life, and moving on to where she was
meant to be, wherever that was.

"Has Dr. MacLean said anything to you?" Liz
asked. "About who he has in mind?" Liz was
curious. She knew a number of childless young
couples who would have been happy to have her
baby.

"He hasn't said anything," Maribeth said with
a look of concern. "I hope he knows I really
mean it. Maybe he thinks Tommy and I . . ."
She hesitated on the words and Liz laughed.

"I think he does. He kind of hinted to me a
while back what a great 'young man' Tom was.
I think he thought the baby was his. At least
that was what I thought when I first found out.
Scared me to death, I'll admit . . . but I don't
know. I suppose there are worse fates. Tommy
seems to be handling it pretty well, even though
it's not his, and that must be even harder."

"He's been fantastic to me," Maribeth said,
feeling closer to his mother than she had felt to
her own in years. She was loving and warm and
intelligent, and she seemed to be coming alive
again after a nightmarish year. She was someone
who had grieved for too long, and knew it.

"What are you going to do for the next two

months?" Liz asked as she poured her a glass of milk and gave her some cookies.

"Just work, I guess. Keep on doing work for school. Wait for the baby to come. It's due Christmas."

"That's awfully soon." Liz looked at her warmly. "If I can do anything to help, I want you to let me know." She wanted to help both of them now, both Maribeth and Tommy, and before Maribeth left late that afternoon, she promised to see what she could do for her at school. The prospect of that filled her with excitement, and Maribeth told Tommy all about it that night when he picked her up and took her to the movies.

They went to see *Bwana Devil*, in 3-D, and they had to wear colored glasses to get the three-dimensional effect. It was the first movie of its kind, and they both loved it. And after that, she told him all about the time she had spent with his mother. Maribeth had a great deal of respect for her, and Liz was growing fonder of her daily. She had invited her to dinner the following weekend. And when Maribeth told Tommy about it, he said that having her around his family sometimes made him feel almost married. He blushed when he said the words, but it was obvious that he liked it. He had been thinking about that a lot lately, now that the baby was coming so much closer.

"That wouldn't be so bad, would it?" he asked, when he took her home, trying to seem casual. "Being married I mean." He looked so young and innocent when he said it. But Maribeth had already promised his mother, and herself, that she wouldn't let him do it.

"Until you got good and sick of me. Like in a year or two, or when I got really old, like twenty-three," she teased. "Think of that, it's seven years from now. We could have eight kids by then, at the rate I'm going." She always had a sense of humor about herself, and about him, but this time she knew he wasn't joking.

"Be serious, Maribeth."

"I am. That's the trouble. We're both too young, and you know it." But he was determined to talk to her about it again. He wasn't going to let her put him off. She still had another two months to go, but before it was all over, he wanted to make her a serious proposal of marriage.

And she was still avoiding it, the following week, when he took her skating. They had just had the first snow, and the lake was shimmering. He couldn't resist going there, and it reminded him of Annie, and all the times he had taken her skating.

"I used to come here on weekends with her. I brought her here the week before . . . she died." He forced himself to say the words, no matter how much they hurt him. He knew it was time to face the fact that she was gone, but it still wasn't easy. "I miss the way she teased me all the time. She was always bugging me

194

about girls . . . she would have driven me crazy about you." He smiled, thinking of his little sister.

When she had gone to their house, Maribeth had seen her room. She had wandered into it accidentally, while looking for the bathroom. And everything was there. Her little bed, her dolls, the cradle she put them in, the bookcase with her books, her pillow and little pink blanket. It tore at Maribeth's heart but she hadn't told any of them that she had seen it. It was like visiting a shrine, and it told her just how much they all missed her.

But she was laughing, listening to him now, as he told her stories about the girls Annie had scared off, mostly because she thought they were too dumb or too ugly.

"I probably wouldn't have made it either, you know," Maribeth said, sliding out on the ice with him, and wondering if she shouldn't. "Especially now. She'd probably have thought I was an elephant. I certainly feel like one," she said, but still looked graceful on the ice in the skates she had borrowed from Julie.

"Should you be doing this?" he asked, suspecting somehow that she shouldn't.

"I'll be fine," she said calmly, "as long as I don't fall," and with that she made a few graceful spins to show him that she hadn't always been a blimp. He was impressed with her ease on the ice, and she made her figure eights look effortless, until suddenly her heel caught, and she fell with a great thud on the ice, and Tommy and several other people looked stunned and then hurried toward her. She had hit her head, and knocked the wind out of herself, and it took three people to get her up, and when they did, she almost fainted. Tommy half carried her off the ice, and everyone looked immensely worried.

"You'd better get her to a hospital," one of the mothers skating with her kids said in an undertone. "She could go into labor." He helped her into the truck, and a moment later was speeding her to Dr. MacLean, while berating her, and himself, for being so stupid.

"How could you do a thing like that?" he asked. "And why did I let you? . . . How do you feel? Are you all right?" He was an absolute wreck by the time they arrived, and she had no labor pains, but she had a good-sized headache.

"I'm fine," she said, looking more than a little sheepish. "And I know it was dumb, but I get so tired of being fat and clumsy, and enormous."

"You're not. You're pregnant. You're supposed to be like that. And just because you don't want the baby, you don't have to kill it." She started to cry when he said that, and by the time they reached Dr. MacLean's, they were both upset, and Maribeth was still crying, while Tommy apologized and then yelled at her again for going skating.

"What happened? What happened? Good heavens, what's going on here?" The doctor couldn't make head or tail of it as they argued.

All he could make out was that Maribeth had hit her head and tried to kill the baby. And then she started crying again, and finally she confessed, and explained that she had taken a spill on the ice when they'd gone skating.

"Skating?" He looked surprised. None of his other patients had tried that one. But they weren't sixteen years old, and both Tommy and Maribeth looked seriously mollified when he gave them a brief lecture. No horseback riding, no ice-skating, no bicycling now, in case she fell off, especially on icy roads, and no skiing. "And no football," he added with a small smile, and Tommy chuckled. "You have to behave yourselves," he said, and then added another sport they were not supposed to indulge in. "And no intercourse again until after the baby." Neither of them explained that they never had, nor that Tommy was a virgin.

"Can I trust you not to go ice-skating again?" The doctor looked at her pointedly, and she looked sheepish.

"I promise." And when Tommy left to get the car, she reminded him again that she was not planning to keep the baby, and she wanted him to find a family to adopt it.

"You're serious about that?" He seemed surprised. The Whittaker boy was so obviously devoted to her. He would have married her in a moment. "Are you sure, Maribeth?"

"I am . . . I think so . . ." she said, trying to sound grown up. "I just can't take care of a baby."

"Wouldn't his family help?" He knew that Liz Whittaker had wanted another baby. But maybe they didn't approve of his son having one so young, and out of wedlock. True to his promise to the kids, he'd never asked them.

But Maribeth's ideas were firm on the subject. "I wouldn't want them to do that. It's not right. This baby has a right to real parents, not children taking care of it. How can I take care of it and go to school? How can I feed it? My parents won't even let me come home, unless I come home without it." She had tears in her eyes as she explained her situation, and by then Tommy had come back again, and the doctor patted her hand, sorry for her. She was too young to shoulder such burdens.

"I'll see what I can do," he said quietly, and then told Tommy to put her to bed for two days. No work, no fun, no sex, no skating.

"Yes, sir," he said, helping her to the car, and holding her tight so she didn't slip on any icy patches. He asked her then what she and the doctor had been talking about. They had both looked very serious when he came back to get her.

"He said he'd help me find a family for the baby." She didn't say anything else to him, and she was startled to realize that he was driving her to his house, not her own. "Where are we going?" she said, still looking upset. It wasn't a happy thought, giving up her baby, even if she knew it was the right thing. She knew it was going to be very painful.

"I called Mom," he explained. "The doctor said you can only get up for meals. Otherwise you have to stay in bed. So I asked Mom if you could spend the weekend."

"Oh no . . . you can't do that . . . I couldn't . . . where would I . . ." She seemed distraught, not wanting to impose on them, but it was all arranged, and his mother hadn't hesitated for a second. Though she had been horrified by how foolish they had been to go skating.

"It's all right, Maribeth," Tommy said calmly. "She said you can stay in Annie's room." There was the faintest catch in his voice as he said it. No one had been in that room in eleven months, but his mother had offered it, and when they arrived, the bed was made, the sheets were fresh, and his mother had a steaming cup of hot chocolate ready.

"Are you all right?" she asked, deeply concerned. Having had several miscarriages, she didn't want anything like that to happen to Maribeth, particularly at this stage. "How could you be so foolhardy? You're lucky she didn't lose the baby," she scolded Tommy. But they were both young, and as she scolded them, they looked like children.

And in the pink nightgown Liz loaned her, in the narrow bed in Annie's room, Maribeth looked more like a little girl than ever. Her bright red hair hung in long braids, and all of Annie's dolls sat gazing at her from around the room. She slept for hours that afternoon, until Liz came to check on her, and ran a hand across her cheek to make sure she didn't have a fever. Liz had called Dr. MacLean herself and been reassured to hear that he didn't think she'd done any harm to the baby.

"They're so young," he smiled as he talked to her, and then said he thought it was too bad she was giving up the baby, but he didn't want to say more. He didn't want Liz to think he was intruding. "She's a nice girl," he said thoughtfully, and Liz agreed, and then went to check on her. Maribeth was just stirring and she said her headache was better. But she still felt guilty about being in that room. More than anything, she didn't want to upset them.

But Liz was surprised how good it felt to be back in Annie's room, sitting on the bed again, and looking into Maribeth's big green eyes. She looked hardly older than Annie.

"How do you feel?" Liz asked her in a whisper. She had slept for almost three hours, while Tommy played ice hockey and left her with his mother.

"Kind of achy, and stiff, but better, I think. I was so scared when I fell. I really thought I might have killed the baby . . . it didn't move at all for a while . . . and Tommy was yelling at me . . . it was awful."

"He was just frightened," she smiled gently at her and tucked her in again, "you both were. It won't be long now. Seven more weeks, Dr.

MacLean said, maybe six." It was an enormous responsibility for her, caring for another human being within her body. "I used to be so excited before my babies came . . . getting everything ready," and then suddenly Liz looked sad for her, realizing that in her case, it would be very different. "I'm sorry," she said, with tears in her eyes, but Maribeth smiled and touched her hand.

"It's okay . . . thank you for letting me stay here . . . I love this room . . . it's funny to say, since we never met, but I really love her. I dream about her sometimes, and all the things Tommy has said about her. I always feel like she's still here . . . in our hearts and our minds . . ." She hoped she wouldn't upset Liz too much by saying that, but the older woman smiled and nodded.

"I feel that too. She's always near me." She seemed more peaceful than she had in a long time, and John did too. Maybe they had finally come around. Maybe they were going to make it. "Tommy says you think that some special people pass through our lives to bring us blessings . . . I like that idea . . . she was here for such a short time . . . five years seems like so little now, but it was such a gift . . . I'm glad I knew her. She taught me so many things . . . about laughing, and loving, and giving."

"That's what I mean," Maribeth said softly, as the two women held hands tightly, across her covers. "She taught you things . . . she even

taught me about Tommy, and I never knew her
. . . and my baby will teach me something too,
even though I'll only know it for a few days . . .
or a few hours." Her eyes filled with tears as she
said it. "And I want to give it the best gift of
all . . . people who will love it." She closed her
eyes and the tears rolled down her cheeks, as
Liz bent to kiss her forehead.

"You will. Now try and sleep some more . . .
you and the baby need it." Maribeth nodded,
unable to say any more, and Liz quietly left the
room. She knew that Maribeth had a hard time
ahead of her, but a time of great gifts too, and
a time of blessings.

Tommy didn't come home until late that afternoon, and asked for her as soon as he came
in. But his mother was quick to reassure him.
"She's fine. She's sleeping." He peeked in at her
then, and she was sound asleep in Annie's bed,
holding one of her dolls, and looking like an
angel.

He looked suddenly grown up as he walked
back out of the room and looked at his mother.

"You love her a lot, Son, don't you?"

"I'm going to marry her one day, Mom," he
said, certain that he meant it.

"Don't make plans yet. Neither of you knows
where life will take you."

"I'll find her. I'll never let her go. I love her
. . . and the baby . . ." he said, sounding determined.

"It's going to be hard for her, giving it up,"

Liz said. She worried for both of them, they had taken so much on. Maribeth by accident, and Tommy out of kindness.

"I know, Mom." And if he had anything to say about it, he wouldn't let her.

When Maribeth walked slowly out of Annie's room at dinnertime, Tommy was at the kitchen table, doing homework. "How do you feel?" he asked, smiling up at her. She looked refreshed and prettier than ever.

"Like I've been much too lazy." She looked at his mother apologetically as she finished dinner. Liz was cooking often these days, and even Tommy loved it.

"Sit down, young lady. You're not supposed to be wandering around. You heard what the doctor said. Bed, or at least a chair. Tommy, push your friend into a chair, please. And no, you may not take her out skating again tomorrow." They both grinned at her like naughty children, and she handed them each a freshly baked chocolate cookie. She liked having young people in the house again. She was happy Tommy had brought her home to them. It was fun having a young girl around. It reminded her that she would never see Annie grown up, and yet she enjoyed being with Maribeth, and so did John. He was happy to find them all in the kitchen when he got home from some unexpected Saturday afternoon work at the office.

"What's going on here? A meeting?" he teased them, pleased to encounter the festive atmosphere in his long-silent kitchen.

"A scolding. Tommy tried to kill Maribeth to-day, he took her skating."

"Oh for heaven's sake . . . why not football?" He looked at him, reminded again of how young they both were. But she seemed to have survived it.

"We thought we'd try football tomorrow, Dad. After hockey."

"Excellent plan." He grinned at both of them, happy that nothing had gone wrong. And after dinner that night, they all played charades and then Scrabble. Maribeth got two seven-letter words, and Liz brought her up to date on the school's position about her assignments. They were willing to give her credit and equivalency, and if she was willing to let Liz give her four exams by the end of the year, they were not only willing to acknowledge completion of her junior year, but roughly half her senior year as well. The work she'd turned in had been first-rate, and if she did well in her exams, she would only have one semester to complete before graduation.

"You did it, kiddo," she congratulated her, proud of her, just as she would have been of one of her students.

"No, I didn't," Maribeth beamed, "you did." And then she let out a happy little squeal and reminded Tommy that she was now a senior.

"Don't let it go to your head. You know, my mom could still flunk you if she wanted. She might too, she's really tough on seniors." They were all in high spirits, even the baby that night. It had gotten its energy back with a vengeance and was kicking Maribeth visibly every five minutes.

"It's mad at you," Tommy said later, as he sat on her bed next to her, and felt the baby kicking. "I guess it should be. That was really dumb of me . . . I'm sorry . . ."

"Don't be, I loved it," Maribeth grinned. She was still elated about the good news of her senior status.

"That means a lot to you, doesn't it? School, I mean," he said, as he watched her face while they talked about school, and not having to go back as a junior.

"I just want to go back, and move on as soon as I can. Even six months will seem like forever."

"Will you come visit?" he asked sadly. He hated thinking about when she'd be gone.

"Sure," she said, but she didn't sound convincing. "I'll try. You can visit me too." But they both suspected that her father wouldn't be giving him the warm welcome she was enjoying from his parents. Just as Tommy had, they were falling in love with her. They could see easily why Tommy loved her. "Maybe I could visit next summer, before I go to Chicago."

"Why Chicago?" he complained, no longer satisfied with just a summer. "Why not go to college here?"

"I'll apply," she conceded, "we'll see if I get accepted."

"With your grades, they'll beg you."

"Not exactly," she grinned, and he kissed her, and they both forgot about grades and school and college and even the baby, although it kicked him soundly as he held her.

"I love you, Maribeth," he reminded her, "both of you. Don't ever forget that." She nodded then, and he held her for a long time, as they sat side by side on his sister's narrow bed, talking quietly about all the things that mattered to them. His parents were already in bed, and they knew he was there. But they trusted them. And eventually, when Maribeth started to yawn, Tommy smiled at her, and then went back to his own room, wondering about their future.

Chapter Eight

Liz invited Maribeth to share Thanksgiving with them, late one afternoon when she was working on a history paper with her. It was an important assignment Liz had designed for her in order to get her senior credit. Maribeth was doing hours of work every night, after she finished work, and sometimes she stayed up until two or three in the morning. But she had a sense of urgency about it all now. She wanted to get all the credits she could before she went back to school. And the work Liz was giving her was going to be her ticket to freedom. She had every intention of finishing high school in June, and then trying to work her way through college. Her father wouldn't like it of course, which was why she wanted to go to Chicago.

But Liz explored the possibility again of her coming back to Grinnell, to attend college there. Wherever Maribeth wanted to go, Liz was willing to write her a recommendation. From the work she'd seen her do, she knew she'd be an asset to any institution. It just struck her as unfortunate that her own family was so unwilling to help her get an education.

"My dad just doesn't think it's important for girls," she said as they put the books away, and Maribeth helped Liz start dinner. It was her day off, and she had even helped Liz correct some simple sophomore papers. "My mom never went to college. I think she should have. She loves to read, loves to learn about things. Dad doesn't even like to see her read the paper. He says women don't need to know those things, it just confuses them. All they need to do is take care of the kids and keep the house clean. He always says you don't need a college education to change a diaper."

"That's certainly simple and direct," Liz said, trying not to sound as furious as it made her. In her opinion, there was no reason why women couldn't do both, be intelligent and educated, and take care of their husbands and children. She was happy she had gone back to work this year. She had forgotten how rewarding it was, and how much she enjoyed it. She had been at home for so long that the pleasures of teaching had somehow faded. But now, with Annie gone, it filled a void she couldn't fill otherwise. An emptiness of time, if nothing else, but she liked seeing those bright, excited faces. It dulled the pain for her sometimes, although the deep ache of their loss never really left her.

She and John still didn't talk about it. They talked about very little these days. There was nothing to say, but at least the words they exchanged seemed a little less sharp, and more than once he had touched her hand, or asked her something in a gentle voice that reminded her of the time before Annie died, and they had lost each other in the process. It seemed that lately, he came home earlier than he had in a long time, and Liz was making an effort to make dinner again. It was almost as though meeting Maribeth had softened all of them, and brought them a little closer. She was so vulnerable, so young, and she and Tommy were so much in love with each other. Sometimes it made Liz smile just to watch them.

She reiterated the invitation to spend Thanksgiving with them as they were cooking dinner.

"I wouldn't want to intrude," Maribeth said, meaning it. She had already planned to volunteer to work at the restaurant, for the few stragglers who came in for a turkey dinner. Most of the other girls had families or kids, and wanted to be home with them. Maribeth had nowhere to be, and thought she might as well work, to help the others. She felt a little guilty now, deserting them, just so she could be with Tommy and his parents, and she said as much to Liz as she set the table.

"You're too far along to be working this hard anyway," Liz scolded her as she put a pot of soup on. "You shouldn't be on your feet all the time." The baby was only a month away, and Maribeth was huge now.

"I don't mind," she said quietly, trying not to think of the baby as much as she was inclined to. It was hard not to think of it. She could feel the flutter of its arms and legs pushing at her, and sometimes it just made her smile to feel it.

"How long are you going to work at the restaurant?" Liz asked, as they sat down for a few minutes.

"Right till the end, I guess." Maribeth shrugged, she needed the money.

"You ought to stop before that," Liz said gently. "At least give yourself a couple of weeks to rest. Even at your age, it's a lot for your body to go through. Besides, I'd like to see you have some real time to spend on your exams when you take them." Liz had scheduled them for mid-December.

"I'll do what I can," Maribeth promised, and the two women chatted about other things as they shared the tasks of preparing dinner. Liz was just turning all the flames down to keep things warm when both Tommy and his father came in, their arrival perfectly timed, their spirits high. Tommy had been helping his dad at work after school, and John had called home for the first time in months, to ask what time they should be home for dinner.

"Hi, girls, what have you been up to?" John asked jovially as he kissed his wife cautiously, and then glanced at her face to see her reaction. Lately, they seemed to be drifting slowly closer again, but it frightened both of them a little. They had been apart for so long, that any intimacy between them seemed unusual and foreign. He glanced at Maribeth with a warm smile too, and saw that Tommy was holding her hand and talking to her quietly at the kitchen table.

They had all had a good day, and Liz gave Tommy the job of talking Maribeth into joining them for Thanksgiving. But it was easily done, when he took her home after they'd done their homework in the living room, and they were sitting in the truck talking. She felt so nostalgic these days, so sensitive about so many things, and sometimes so frightened. Suddenly she wanted to cling to him, and hold on to him in ways she had never expected. She wanted to be with him more than she had before, and she always felt relieved and happy when he walked into the restaurant, or her room, or his parents' kitchen.

"Are you okay?" he asked her gently, as he saw she had tears in her eyes when she said she'd come for Thanksgiving.

"Yeah, I'm fine," she looked embarrassed as she wiped the tears away. "Just stupid, I guess. I don't know . . . things just make me cry now . . . they're so nice to me, and they don't even know me. Your mom has helped me with school, with everything . . . they've done so much for me, and I don't know how to thank them."

"Marry me," he said seriously, and she laughed.

"Yeah, sure. That would really do it. They'd really thank me for that one."

"I think they would. You're the best thing that's happened to my family in years. My parents haven't even spoken to each other all year, except to yell at each other, or say something mean about not putting gas in the car, or forgetting to let the dog out. They love you, Maribeth. We all do."

"That's no reason to wreck your life, just because I made a mess of my own. They're just very nice people."

"So am I," he said, holding her tight, refusing to let her go, while she giggled. "You'll like me even better when we're married."

"You're crazy."

"Yeah," he grinned, "about you. You can't get rid of me this easy."

"I don't want to," she said, her eyes filling with tears again, and then she laughed at herself. She seemed to be on a roller coaster of emotions, but Dr. MacLean had told her it was normal. She was in her last month, and a lot of major changes were about to happen. And particularly at her age, and in her situation, a lot of emotional ups and downs were to be expected.

Tommy walked her slowly to the door, and they lingered for a long time on the steps. It was a clear cold night and when he kissed her good night he could feel her and the baby and he knew he wanted her forever. He refused to accept the idea that she might never marry him, or sleep with him, or have his baby. He wanted to share so much with her, and he knew he would never let her go now, he kissed her again and then left her finally as he hurried down the steps looking handsome and tousled.

"What are you looking so happy about?" his mother asked as he came in after he took Maribeth home.

"She's coming to Thanksgiving," he said, but she could see that there was more than that. He was living on dreams and hopes, and the excitement of first love. Sometimes he was so elated when he'd been with her he was almost manic.

"Did she say anything else?" His mother watched him carefully. She worried about him sometimes, she knew how much he was in love with her. But she also knew that Maribeth had bigger problems. Giving up a child was liable to mark her forever. "How is she coping with things? It's getting awfully close to her due date." She was healthy, but in her case, that wasn't the problem. She had childbirth to face, with no husband, no family, a baby to give up, if she really did, and a difficult family situation to go home to. She was adamant about leaving them by June, if she even made it that long, which Liz sometimes doubted. She'd been gone for five months, and had been completely independent of them. It wouldn't be easy for her to go back now, and take whatever abuse her father chose to dish out for her transgressions.

"Is she really serious about giving up the baby?" Liz asked, as she finished drying the dishes, and Tommy munched on some cookies. He liked talking to his mother, she knew about things, and girls, and life. They hadn't talked much in the last year, but she seemed more like her old self now.

"I think she is. I think she's crazy to do it. But she says she knows she can't take care of it right. I don't think she really wants to give it up, but she thinks she should, for the baby's sake."

"The ultimate sacrifice," Liz said sadly, thinking that there was nothing worse in the world for any woman to face, and wishing she could have another baby.

"I keep telling her not to, but she won't listen."

"Maybe she's right. For her. Maybe she knows what she can and can't do right now. She's very young, and she has no one to help her. Her family doesn't sound as though they'll do anything for her. It would be a terrible burden, and she might hold it against the child. It might ruin both their lives if she kept it." She couldn't imagine it, but in all fairness she had to admit that Maribeth's situation was anything but easy.

"That's what she says. She says she knows it's the right thing for her to do. I think that's why she doesn't talk about the baby much, or buy little baby things. She doesn't want to get attached to it." But he still wanted to marry her and keep it. To him, that seemed the right thing to do. He was willing to shoulder his own responsibilities, hers, and someone else's. His parents had taught him well, and he was an exceptionally decent person.

"You have to listen to what she wants, Tom," Liz warned. "She knows what's right for her, no matter how it seems to you. Don't try to force her into something else . . ." she looked at him pointedly then ". . . or yourself into something you can't handle. You're both very young, marriage and parenthood isn't something to be entered into lightly, or because you want to help someone out. It's a nice thought, but it's a lot to live up to. If things go wrong, and they do sometimes, you both have to be very strong to help each other. You can't do that at sixteen," . . . or even at forty or fifty . . . she and John had done so little to help each other in the past year. She realized now how lonely they had both been, how alone, and unable to support each other. They had been totally lost to each other.

"I love her, Mom," he said honestly, feeling something wrench at his heart. "I don't want her to go through all that alone." He was being honest with her, and she knew him well. She knew what he wanted to do for Maribeth, and however good his intentions were, or how sweet Maribeth was, she didn't want them to get married. Not yet, not now, and not for the wrong reasons.

"She's not alone. You're there for her."

"I know. But it's not the same," he said sadly.

"She needs to work this out. It's her life too. Let her find the right road for herself. If it's right for you both, one day you'll be together."

He nodded, wanting to convince all of them

that she should keep the baby and marry him, but even Maribeth wouldn't agree to that, nor his parents. They were all being incredibly stubborn.

But on Thanksgiving they looked like one happy family, as they sat around the table. Liz had used their best lace tablecloth that had been John's grandmother's and a wedding present to them, and the china they only used on special occasions. Maribeth wore a dark green silk dress she'd bought for the holidays, and her thick red hair cascaded in generous waves past her shoulders. Her big green eyes made her look like a little girl, and in spite of her vast girth, she looked incredibly pretty. Liz had worn a bright blue dress, and a touch of rouge, which no one had seen in a long time. The men wore suits, and the house looked warm and festive.

Maribeth had brought flowers to Liz, big gold chrysanthemums, and a box of chocolates, which Tommy was devouring. And after lunch, when they all sat in front of the fireplace, they seemed more of a family than ever. It was their first major holiday without Annie, and Liz had been dreading it. And she'd thought of her repeatedly that day, but somehow with Maribeth and Tommy near at hand, it didn't seem quite as painful. And that afternoon, Liz and John went for a long walk, and Tommy took Maribeth for a drive. Although she had offered to work, they had given her the weekend off work, and she was staying with Tommy and his parents.

"No skating, you two!" Liz called as they drove off, and she and John walked along with the dog. They were going to drop in on some friends, and the foursome had agreed to meet back at the house in two hours and go to a movie.

"What do you want to do?" Tom asked as they drove toward the lake, but Maribeth had an odd request. He was surprised, but in some ways relieved. He had wanted to go there all day, and thought she would think he was weird and crazy if he said it.

"Would you mind terribly if we stopped at the cemetery for a few minutes? I just thought . . . I felt like I was taking her place today, except I wasn't. I kept wishing she was there with us, so your parents would be happy again. I don't know . . . I just want to stop and say hi to her."

"Yeah," Tommy said, "me too." It was exactly what he had felt, except that his parents had been a lot better than they had been in a long time, especially with each other.

They stopped and bought flowers along the way. Little yellow and pink sweetheart roses with baby's breath, tied with long pink ribbons, and they set them gently on her grave, next to the little white marble headstone.

"Hi, kiddo," Tommy said quietly, thinking of the big blue eyes that had always sparkled. "Mom made a pretty good turkey today. You'd have hated the stuffing, it had raisins."

They sat there together for a long time, holding hands, thinking about her, and not talking. It was hard to believe that she'd been gone almost a year. In some ways it seemed only moments since she left, in other ways it felt like forever.

"Bye, Annie," Maribeth said softly as they left, but they both knew that they took her with them. She went with them everywhere, in the memories Tommy carried with him, in the room where Maribeth stayed, in the look in Liz's eyes when she remembered.

"She was such a great kid," he said with a catch in his voice as he walked away. "I still can't believe she's gone."

"She isn't," Maribeth said softly. "You just can't see her now, Tommy. But she's always with you."

"I know," he shrugged, looking all of sixteen, and not an instant more, "but I still miss her."

Maribeth nodded, and moved closer to him. The holidays made her think of her family, and talking about Annie made her miss Noelle. She hadn't been able to speak to her since she left home, and her mother had told her months before on the phone that her father wouldn't let Noelle have Maribeth's letters. At least she'd be seeing her soon . . . but what if something ever happened to her . . . like Annie . . . the very thought of it made her shudder.

Maribeth was quiet when they got home, and Tommy knew she was upset about something. He wondered if maybe he shouldn't have taken

218

her to Annie's grave. Maybe at this stage in her pregnancy, it was too upsetting.

"Are you okay? Do you want to lie down?"

"I'm fine," she said, fighting back tears again. His parents weren't home yet. He and Maribeth had come back early. And then she totally surprised him. "Do you think your parents would mind if I called home? I just thought that maybe . . . maybe on the holiday . . . I just thought I'd say Happy Thanksgiving."

"Sure . . . that's fine." He was sure his parents wouldn't mind. And if they did, he'd pay for the call himself. He left her alone while she gave the operator her number, and waited.

Her mother was the first to come on the line. She sounded breathless and busy, and there was a lot of noise around her. Maribeth knew that her aunts and their families always went to her house for Thanksgiving, and both of them had young children. There was lots of squealing, and her mother couldn't hear her.

"Who? . . . stop that! I can't hear! Who is it?"

"It's me, Mom," Maribeth said a little louder. "Maribeth. I wanted to wish you a Happy Thanksgiving."

"Oh my God!" she said, and burst instantly into tears. "Your father will kill me."

"I just wanted to say hi, Mom." She suddenly wanted to touch her and hold her and hug her. She hadn't realized until then how much she had missed her. "I miss you, Mom." Tears swam in her eyes, and Margaret Robertson almost keened as she listened.

"Are you all right?" she asked in an under-voice, hoping that no one would hear her. "Have you had it yet?"

"Not for another month." But as she answered, there was a sudden outburst at the other end, an argument, and the phone was wrenched from her mother's hand, and a sharp voice came over the line clearly.

"Who is this?" he barked. He could tell from his wife's tears who was calling.

"Hi, Daddy. I just wanted to wish you a Happy Thanksgiving." Her hand trembled violently, but she tried to sound normal.

"Is it over? You know what I mean?" He sounded merciless and brutal as she fought back tears.

"Not yet . . . I just . . . I wanted to . . ."

"I told you not to call here until it's over. Come home when you've taken care of everything and gotten rid of it. And don't call us until then. Do you hear?"

"I hear, I . . . Daddy, please . . ." She could hear her mother crying in the background, and she thought she heard Noelle shrieking at him, telling him he couldn't do that, but he did, and as Maribeth cried, he put down the receiver, and the operator came back on the line and asked if she was finished.

She was crying too hard to even answer her. She just put down the phone, and sat there, looking like a lost child, and sobbing. Tommy came back into the room and was horrified to see the state she was in. "What happened?"

"He wouldn't . . . let me . . . talk to Mom . . ." she sobbed, "and he told me not to call again until I'd 'gotten rid of it.' He . . . I . . ." She couldn't even tell him what she was feeling, but it was easy to see. And she was still upset when his parents came home half an hour later. He had made her lie down, because she was crying so hard, he thought she'd have the baby.

"What happened?" his mother asked, looking concerned when he told her.

"She called her parents, and her father hung up on her. I guess she was talking to her mom, and he grabbed the phone, and told her not to call them again until after she'd given up the baby. They sound awful, Mom. How can she go back there?"

"I don't know," Liz said, looking worried. "He certainly doesn't sound like much of a father. But she seems to be very attached to her mom . . . it'll only be till June . . ." But Liz had a very clear picture that it was going to be rough on Maribeth when she went back to her parents.

She walked quietly into Annie's room, and sat down on the bed next to Maribeth, who was still crying.

"You can't let him upset you like that," she said calmly, holding Maribeth's hand in her own, and gently stroking her fingers, just as she had Annie's. "It's not good for you, or the baby."

"Why does he have to be so mean? Why can't he at least let me talk to Noelle and Mom?" She didn't care if she didn't talk to Ryan, he was just like their father.

"He thinks he's protecting them from your mistakes. He doesn't understand. He's probably embarrassed by what happened."

"So am I. That doesn't change how I feel about them."

"I don't think he understands that. You're a lucky girl, you have a fine mind, and a big heart. You have a future, Maribeth. He doesn't."

"What future do I have? Everyone in town will always talk about what happened. They'll know. Even though I went away, people will talk, someone will tell them. And they'll hate me. Guys will think I'm easy, girls will think I'm cheap. My dad'll never let me go to college when I finish school. He'll try and make me work for him at the shop, or stay home and help my mom, and I'll get buried just like she did."

"You don't have to," Liz said quietly. "You don't have to do anything the way she did. And you know who you are. You know you're not easy or cheap. You'll finish school and then decide what you want . . . and you'll do it."

"He won't let me talk to them again. I'll never be able to talk to my mom again." She began sobbing again, like a small child, and Liz held her in her arms and hugged her. It was all she could do, just be there for her. It broke her heart to see this wonderful girl go back to those mis-

222

erable people. She could see now why Tommy wanted to marry her. It was all he could think of doing to help her. Liz wanted to just keep her there, and keep her safe from them. But on the other hand, they were her family, and Liz knew that in her own way she missed them. Maribeth always talked about going home after the baby. She may not have known what she should do, but she always wanted to see them.

"He'll be better once you're home," Liz said, trying to encourage her, but Maribeth only shook her head and blew her nose in Liz's hankie.

"No he won't. He'll be worse. He'll remind me of it all the time, just like he does my aunts. He always makes comments about how they had to get married, and they get all embarrassed. Or at least one of them does. She used to cry all the time. The other one told him off, and told him her husband would beat him up if he ever mentioned it again. And actually, he doesn't say anything about her now."

"Maybe there's a lesson to be learned," Liz said, thinking about it. "Maybe you need to make it clear that you won't take it." But she was a sixteen-year-old girl. How could she stand up to her father? It was just lucky for her she had found the Whittakers. Without them, she'd have been completely alone and having this baby.

Liz helped her get up again after a little while, and made her a cup of tea, while the two men talked quietly and sat in front of the fire. And eventually, they went to the movie anyway, and Maribeth was in better spirits by the time they came back. No one mentioned her parents again, and when they got home, they all went to bed early.

"I feel so sorry for her," Liz said to John, once they were in bed. They were friendlier again, and they talked more openly about things now. There wasn't the same deafening silence in their bedroom.

"Tommy feels sorry for her too," he said. "It's a damn shame she got pregnant." That much was obvious, but Liz was just as upset about her parents.

"I hate to see her go home to them, and yet in a funny way she wants to."

"They're all she's got. And she's very young. But it won't last. She wants to go to college, and her father can't handle it."

"He sounds like a real tyrant. But he gets away with it. Maybe if someone talked to him . . ." Liz said pensively. "She needs a way out, an alternative, so if things don't work out there, she has somewhere else to go to."

"I don't want her marrying Tommy," he said firmly. "At least not yet. They're too young, and she's made a big mistake and needs to get over it. It's too much for him to take on now, even though he wants to."

"I know that," she snapped at John. Sometimes he still annoyed her. Neither of them wanted Tommy married now, but she wasn't prepared to abandon Maribeth either. She had crossed their path for a reason, and she was a remarkable girl. Liz was not going to turn her back on her, or fail to help her.

"I think you ought to stay out of it. She'll have the baby, and go home to them. If she has a problem, she can always call us. I'm sure Tommy will stay in touch with her. He's crazy about the girl. He's not going to just forget her the minute she leaves here." Even though the distance between their homes would provide something of a challenge for them to continue their romance.

"I want to talk to them," Liz said, suddenly looking at him, and he shook his head. "I mean her parents."

"Don't meddle in their affairs."

"They're not 'their' affairs, they're hers. Those people have left her to solve her own problems at a time when she really needs them. They've left her completely to her own devices. As I see it, they've lost their right to dictate the terms, based on their failure to support her."

"They may not see it that way." He smiled, sometimes he loved the way she got involved, and cared so much about everything, and sometimes she drove him crazy. She hadn't cared about anything in a long time, and he was glad in a way that Maribeth had sparked that in her again. She had sparked a lot of things, in all of them. In some ways, he felt fatherly toward her.

"Let me know what you decide," he said, smiling again as she turned off the light.

"Will you come with me if I go to see them?" she asked bluntly. "I want to see them for myself before she goes back there," Liz said, feeling unusually maternal toward Maribeth. Maybe one day, she might even be her daughter-in-law, but whether she was or not, she was not going to just abandon her to unfeeling parents.

"Actually, I'd like that." He grinned at her in the dark. "I think I'd enjoy watching you give him a piece of your mind." He chuckled and she laughed. "Just let me know when you want to go," he said quietly, and she nodded.

"I'll call them tomorrow," she said thoughtfully, and then she turned on her side and looked at her husband. "Thanks, John." They were friends again, nothing more. But that was at least something.

Chapter Nine

With much regret, Maribeth gave them notice at the restaurant the Monday after Thanksgiving. She and Liz had talked about it again, and she had agreed that she needed time to prepare properly for her exams, and the baby was due right after Christmas. She was going to leave work on the fifteenth, and the Whittakers wanted her to come and stay with them from then until the baby was born. Liz said she shouldn't be alone, in case something happened. And they assured her that they really wanted her with them.

She was overwhelmed by the kindness they had offered her, and she liked the idea of staying with them. She was getting nervous about the delivery now, and staying with them meant she could do more work with Liz, and maybe even get more credits toward school. Not to mention being closer to Tommy. It seemed like an ideal arrangement, and Liz had convinced John that having her there until the baby came was something special they could do for Tommy.

"And she'll need someone to be with her afterwards," Liz explained. "It'll be awfully hard for her with the baby gone." She knew how much pain that would cause her. Having lost her child, she understood only too well what it would cost Maribeth to give up her baby. The agony would be intense, and Liz wanted to be there for her. Without thinking about it, she had come to love the girl, and the bond between them had grown as they worked together. Maribeth had a remarkable mind, and she was tireless in her efforts to improve it. It was something she wanted desperately. It was her only hope for a future.

Everyone at the restaurant was sad that she was moving on. But they understood. She said that she was going back to her family to have the baby but she had never told anyone that she'd never actually been married, or that she wasn't planning to keep the baby. And on her last day there, Julie gave a little shower for her, and everyone brought her little gifts for the baby. There were little booties and a sweater set one of the girls had knitted for her, a pink and blue blanket with little ducks on it, a teddy bear, some toys, a box of diapers from one of the bus-boys, and Jimmy had bought her a high chair.

And as she looked at all the little things they'd given her, Maribeth was overwhelmed with emotion. The sheer kindness of it tore at her heart, but even more than that the realization that she'd never see her child use any of it brought home to her for the first time what it really meant to give up the baby. The baby was suddenly real to her as it had never been before. It had clothes and socks and hats and diapers and a teddy bear and a high chair. What it didn't have was a daddy and a mommy, and when she got back to her room that afternoon, she called Dr. MacLean and asked what progress he'd made in locating adoptive parents for the baby.

"I've had three couples in mind," he said cautiously, "but I'm not sure one of them is the right one." The father had admitted that he had a drinking problem and Avery MacLean was loath to give them a baby. "The second ones just found out that they got pregnant on their own. And the third family may not want to adopt. I haven't talked to them yet. We still have some time."

"Two weeks, Dr. MacLean . . . two weeks . . ." She didn't want to bring the baby home, and then give it away. That would be torture. And she knew she couldn't go home to the Whittakers with a baby. That would be too much of an imposition.

"We'll find someone, Maribeth. I promise. And if not, you can leave the baby at the hospital for a couple of weeks. We'll find the right couple. We don't want to make a mistake, do we?" She agreed with him but the high chair in the corner of her room suddenly seemed ominous. They had all made her promise to call and tell them what sex the baby was, and she had said she would. And knowing that she had lied to all of them made it all the harder to say goodbye, especially to Julie.

"You take care of yourself, you hear!" Julie had admonished her. "I still think you ought to marry Tommy." Maybe she would after the baby came, they all said after she left. And Dr. MacLean was still wondering the same thing when they hung up. He didn't want to help her give the baby up, only to find that she and Tommy would regret it later. He had thought of discussing it with Liz, to see what she thought about it, if they were really serious about giving the baby up, but he wasn't sure how the young couple would feel about his talking to Tommy's parents. It was a sensitive situation. But he could sense Maribeth's urgency now. It was clear that she wanted some resolution, and he promised her, and himself, that he'd launch a serious search for adoptive parents.

The day after she left the restaurant, Tommy helped her move all her things into Annie's room. She put the baby's things that they'd given her in boxes in the garage, and said she'd send them to the hospital for the adoptive parents. It still made her feel choked up to look at them. It made it all seem much too real.

On Saturday morning, Liz explained that she and John had to go out of town until the next day. He needed to look at some produce markets across the state line, and they wouldn't be back until Sunday. She was faintly uncomfortable about leaving them alone, but she and John had discussed it at length and knew they could be trusted.

Tommy and Maribeth were grateful for the time alone, and had every intention of behaving themselves, and not letting his parents down. And as pregnant as Maribeth was, there were no serious temptations.

On Saturday afternoon, they went Christmas shopping. She bought his mother a small cameo pin, it was expensive for her, but she thought it was very beautiful and looked like something she'd wear, and she bought his father a special pipe for bad weather. And as they wandered through the stores, she looked at some baby things, but she always forced herself to put them back and not to buy them.

"Why don't you buy it something from you? Like a teddy bear, or a little locket or something?" He wondered if doing that might get it out of her system, and it would be something she could send with it to its new life and new parents, but her eyes filled with tears as she shook her head. She didn't want any trace of herself on the child. She might be tempted to look for it then, or look searchingly at every child she saw wearing a locket.

"I have to let go, Tommy. Completely. I can't hold on to it." A little sob caught in her throat as she said it.

"Some things you can't let go of," he said, looking at her meaningfully, and she nodded. She didn't want to let go of him, or the baby, but sometimes life made you give up what you loved most. Sometimes there were no compromises or bargains. He knew that too. But he had already lost more than he ever wanted to. And he was not willing to give Maribeth up, or her baby.

They went home with their packages, and she cooked dinner for him. His parents weren't due back till the following afternoon. And it was like being married, fussing over him, and cleaning up the dishes afterwards, and then sitting down to watch television. They watched *Your Show of Shows*, followed by *Hit Parade*. And as they sat there side by side like young newlyweds, Maribeth looked over at him and giggled, and he pulled her onto his lap and kissed her.

"I feel like I'm already married to you," he said, loving it, and feeling the baby kick as he held her and rubbed her stomach. They were surprisingly intimate, considering that they had never made love. But it was hard to remember sometimes that they hadn't. She could feel him springing to life then as she sat on his lap, and she kissed him and felt him grow harder. He was after all only sixteen, and almost everything she did made him horny.

"I don't think you're supposed to get excited over four-hundred-pound girls," she teased, and then got up and walked across the room, rubbing her back, which was achy. They had walked a lot that afternoon, and lately the baby seemed to be a lot lower. There was no doubt that it was going to be born soon, or that it was going to be a very big baby. She was a tall girl, but her hips were narrow, and she had always been thin. Maribeth was beginning to panic every time she thought about giving birth to a baby.

She admitted it to him that night, and he felt sorry for her. He just hoped it wouldn't be as bad as they both feared.

"You probably won't even feel it," he said, handing her a dish of ice cream, which they shared with two spoons.

"I hope not," she agreed, trying to forget her fears. "What do you want to do tomorrow?"

"Why don't we get the tree, and decorate it before Mom and Dad come home? It might be a nice surprise for them." She liked the idea, she liked doing things for them, and being part of their family. And that night when she went to bed in Annie's room, Tommy sat next to her for a long time, and then lay beside her on the narrow bed that had been Annie's. "We could sleep in my parents' room, you know. We'd have enough room and they'd never know it." But they had promised they'd be good, and Maribeth wanted to hold him to it.

"Yes, they would," she said firmly. "Parents know everything."

"That's what my mom thinks," he grinned. "Come on, Maribeth. We won't get another chance. They go away about once every five years."

"I don't think your mom would want us sleeping in her bed," she said primly.

"Okay, then sleep in mine. It's bigger than this," he complained, rolling toward the floor for the tenth time, while she giggled. They didn't have to sleep together at all, but they both wanted to. It was so cozy being together.

"All right." She followed him into his room, and they snuggled up in his bed, in her night-gown and his pajamas, with their arms around each other, giggling and talking, like two kids, and then he kissed her, long and slow and hard, and they both got aroused, but two weeks before her baby was due, there was very little they could do about it. He kissed her breasts and she moaned, and she fondled him, and he was so hard and stiff that he was actually in pain as she held him. And she kept reminding herself that what they were doing was wrong, except that they didn't really think so. It didn't feel wrong to be with him, it felt like the only place she ever wanted to be, for the rest of time, and as she lay there with him, feeling her belly between them, she wondered for the first time if one day they would really be together.

"This is how I want it to be," he said, as he held her in his arms, and they both started to get sleepy. They had stayed aroused for as long as they could stand, and had finally agreed that they had to calm down and stop playing. All their antics had even started to give her contrac-tions. "I just want to be with you for the rest of my life," he said sleepily, "and one day the baby in your belly will be ours, Maribeth . . . that's what I want . . ."

"So do I . . ." She meant it but she wanted other things too, just as his mother had, before she married his father.

"I can wait for you. My dad waited for my mom. Not too long though," he said, thinking of how good it felt when she held him. "Like a year or two," he grinned at her, and then kissed her. "We could get married and go to college together."

"And live on what?"

"We could live here," he said. "We could go to college right here and live with my parents." But she didn't like that idea, no matter how much she loved his parents.

"When we get married, if we do," she said sternly as she yawned, "I want us to be grown-ups, to take care of our own responsibilities, our own kids, however old we have to be to do it."

"Yeah, like maybe sixty," he said, yawning too, as he grinned at her and then kissed her. "I just want you to know, I'm going to marry you one day, Maribeth Robertson. Get used to it. That's all there is to it."

She didn't object, she only smiled, as she lay in his arms, and drifted off to sleep, thinking of Annie, and Tommy, and her baby.

Chapter Ten

They got up early the next day and went to buy the tree, and Tommy bought a little, smaller tree too, a tiny one, that he put in the truck with the big one. He got the decorations out when they got home, and they spent most of the afternoon putting them on the tree. Some of them brought tears to his eyes when he looked at them, mostly the ones that his mother had made with Annie.

"Do you think we should leave them put away?" Maribeth said thoughtfully, and they debated. Seeing them might really upset his mom, but knowing they weren't there would make everyone sad too. There was no easy solution. In the end, they decided to put them up anyway, because leaving them put away would be like denying Annie. She had been there with them, they all shared memories of her. It was better to acknowledge them than to try to pretend they had never existed. And by three o'clock they both agreed that the tree looked good, and it was finished.

She had made him tuna sandwiches for lunch, and as they put the rest of the decorations away, Tommy kept a small box out, and he looked up at Maribeth strangely.

"Is something wrong?"

He shook his head. She could see he was

thinking about something. "No. I've got to go somewhere. Want to come, or are you too tired?"

"I'm okay. What is it?"

"You'll see." He got out their coats, and it was starting to snow as they went out to his truck, and he took the small box of decorations. The tiny tree was still in the back of the truck, and he put the box in beside it. She wasn't sure what he was doing at first, but as soon as they got there, she knew what he had come to do. They were at the cemetery, and he had wanted to bring a little tree to Annie.

He took the tree out of the back of the truck, and she carried the box of decorations. They were the smallest ones, the ones Annie had loved, with little teddy bears, and toy soldiers blowing horns, and tiny angels. There was a string of beads, and a length of silver tinsel. And solemnly, he stood the tree on the ground next to her, in a little wooden stand, and one by one they took turns putting on the decorations. It was a heart-wrenching ritual and it only took a few minutes to complete it, and they stood looking at it, as he remembered how much she had loved Christmas. Annie had loved everything about it. He had told Maribeth about it before, but this time he couldn't say anything. He just stood there, with tears rolling down his cheeks, remembering how much he had loved her, and how much it hurt when he lost her.

He looked up at Maribeth then, from across

the tree, her huge belly swathed in her coat, her eyes so gentle, her bright hair peeking out of the wool scarf she wore. He had never loved her more than at this moment.

"Maribeth," he said softly, knowing that Annie would approve of what he was doing. It was right to do it here. She would have wanted to be part of his life, and his future. "Marry me . . . please . . . I love you . . ."

"I love you too," she said, coming closer to him, and taking his hand in her own as she looked at him, "but I can't . . . not now . . . don't ask me to do that . . ."

"I don't want to lose you . . ." He looked down at the small grave where his sister lay, just beneath them, next to the Christmas tree they had brought for her, "I lost her . . . I don't want to lose you . . . please, let's get married."

"Not yet," she said softly, wanting to give him everything, yet afraid to hurt him if she failed him. She was wiser than her years, and in some ways, wiser than he was.

"Will you promise to marry me later?"

"I promise you solemnly on this day, Thomas Whittaker, that I will love you forever." And she meant every word as she said it. She knew she would never forget what he had been to her ever since the first moment she'd met him. But what that meant, where their lives would lead, no one could promise that, or know now. She wanted to be part of his life forever, but who knew where life would take them?

"Will you promise to marry me?"

"If it's right, if it's what we both want." She was always honest.

"I'll always be there for you," he said solemnly, and she knew he meant it.

"And I for you. I'll always be your friend, Tommy . . . I'll always love you." And if they were lucky, she would be his wife one day. She wanted that too, now, at sixteen, but she was wise enough to know that one day things might be different. Or maybe not, perhaps their love would grow in time, and one day be stronger than ever. Or perhaps like leaves, life's winds would blow them to the far corners of the earth and scatter them forever, but she hoped not.

"I'll be ready to marry you, whenever you want," he affirmed.

"Thank you," she said, and reached up to kiss him. He kissed her, wishing she would promise him everything, but satisfied that she had given him what she could at the moment.

They stood silently, looking at the small Christmas tree then, and thinking about his sister. "I think she loves you too," he said quietly. "I wish she could be here," and then he tucked Maribeth's hand into his arm, and led her back to the truck. It had grown colder since they had first come out, and they were both very quiet on the drive back to his house. There was something very peaceful between them now, something very strong and very clean, and very honest. And they both knew that they might be together one day, or they might not. They would try, they would be there for each other for as long as they could. At sixteen, that was a lot, more than some people had after a lifetime. They had hope, and promise, and dreams. It was a good way to start out. It was a gift they had given each other.

They sat talking quietly in the living room, looking at old albums, and laughing at baby pictures of him, and Annie. And Maribeth had dinner waiting when his parents came home from their trip. His parents were happy to be home and pleased to see them, and excited to see the Christmas tree, and Liz stopped and looked at it long and hard when she saw the familiar decorations, and then she looked at her son and smiled.

"I'm glad you put those on. I would have missed them if they weren't there." It would have been like trying to forget she had ever existed, and Liz didn't want to forget that.

"Thanks, Mom." He was glad they had done the right thing, and they all went into the kitchen to have dinner. Maribeth asked about their trip, and Liz said it had gone well. She didn't look thrilled, but John nodded agreement. It had gone as well as it could have, given the circumstances. But they seemed pleased, and there was a festive atmosphere between them for the rest of the evening. Liz noticed something different about them though. They seemed more serious than they ever had before, and quieter, and they

240

looked at each other with an even stronger bond than Liz had ever noticed between them.

"You don't suppose they did anything while we were gone, do you, John?" she asked him that night, in their room, and he looked amused.

"If you mean what I think you mean, even a sixteen-year-old boy couldn't overcome an obstacle like that one. I'd say your fears are definitely unfounded."

"You don't think they got married, do you?"

"They'd need our permission to do that. Why?"

"They just look different to me. Closer somehow, more like one than two, the way married people are, or are supposed to be." The trip had been good for them too. Being alone in a hotel room had brought them closer than they'd been in years, and he'd taken her out for a very nice dinner. And they had accomplished more or less what they wanted before that.

"I think they're just very much in love. We have to accept that," John said calmly.

"Do you suppose they really will get married one day?"

"It wouldn't be the worst thing for either of them. And they've already been through a lot together. It may prove to be too much for them, in the end, or it might be the making of them. Only time will tell. They're both good kids, I hope they do stay together."

"She wants to wait though," Liz said, understanding that well, and he smiled ruefully.

"I know about that kind of woman." But it was a good kind, as time had proven to him. Not always an easy kind, but a good one. "If it's meant to be, they'll find a way to make it work eventually. If not, they'll have had something most people never have in a whole lifetime. In some ways, I envy them." There was something about starting out again that appealed to him, about having a new life and a clean slate. He would have loved to start fresh with Liz. But for them, in some ways, it was too late now.

"I don't envy her what she'll have to go through," Liz said sadly.

"You mean the delivery?" He sounded surprised, Liz had never complained much about childbirth.

"No, I mean giving the baby up. That won't be easy." He nodded, sorry for her. Sorry for both of them for the pains they would have to go through, growing up, yet still envying them what they shared and had to look forward to, separately or together.

Liz lay close to John that night, as he slept, and Maribeth and Tommy sat and talked for hours in the living room.

They felt exactly what his mother had seen, closer, and more one than two. They were each more than they had ever been. And for the first time in her life, Maribeth felt as though she had a future.

The alarm woke everyone up the next day, and Maribeth showered and dressed in time to help Liz serve breakfast. Liz had arranged for Maribeth to take a special exam to skip the first half of her senior year. And Tommy had finals that day too. They talked about their exams back and forth over the table. The school was letting her take them in a special room, in the administration building, where none of the students would see her, and Liz was going to meet her there for the tests that morning. The school had been incredibly decent to her, they were doing everything they could to help her, thanks to Liz going to bat for her. And when they left each other outside the school, Tommy wished her luck, and then hurried off to his classes.

The rest of the week seemed to fly by, and the next weekend was the last before Christmas. Liz finished her Christmas shopping, and on her way home, she hesitated for a moment, and then turned around and decided to go and see Annie. She had been postponing it for months, because it was too painful for her, and yet today, she felt that she had to.

She drove through the gates of the cemetery, and found the place where they had left her, and as she approached, she stopped and gasped when she saw it. She saw the little tree, listing slightly to one side, the ornaments tinkling in the wind, just as they had left them. She walked slowly up to it, and straightened it, tucking the tinsel in again, looking at the familiar ornaments Annie had hung on their tree only the year before. Her little hands had so carefully put them just where she wanted, and now her mother re-membered every word, every sound, every mo-ment, every silent agony of the past year, and yet suddenly it was a bittersweet kind of pain as she felt the floodgates open and engulf her. She stood there silently for a long time, crying for her little girl, and looking at the tree Maribeth and Tommy had brought her. She touched the prickly branches then, like a little friend, and whispered her name . . . just the sound of it touched her heart like baby fingers.

"I love you, little girl . . . I always will . . . sweet, sweet Annie . . ." She couldn't say good-bye to her, knew she never would again, and she went home feeling sad, and yet strangely peace-ful.

No one was home when she got there, and she was relieved. Liz sat alone in the living room for a long time, looking at their tree, seeing the familiar ornaments there. It was going to be hard having Christmas without her. It was hard every day. It was hard having breakfast and lunch and dinner and trips to the lake or anywhere without their little girl. It was hard getting up in the morning and knowing she wouldn't be there. And yet she knew they had to go on. She had come to visit them, for a short time, if only they had known it would be that way. But what would they have done differently? Would they have loved her more? Given her more things? Spent more time with her? They had done all they could then, but as Liz sat dreaming of her,

she knew she would have given an entire lifetime
for another kiss, another hug, another moment
with her daughter.

She was still sitting there, thinking of her when
the children came home, full of life, their faces
bright red and icy cold, full of stories about
where they'd been and what they'd been doing.

She smiled at them then, and Tommy could
see she had been crying.

"I just want to thank you two," she said, choking on her own words, "for taking the tree to
. . . thank you . . ." she said softly, and walked
away quickly. Maribeth and Tommy didn't
know what to say to her, and Maribeth was crying too, as she took off her coat and hung up
their things. Sometimes she wished she could
make it all better for them. They still all hurt
so much from losing Annie.

His father came home a little while after that,
his arms laden with packages, and Liz was in
the kitchen by then, making dinner. And she
smiled when she looked up to see him. There
was more warmth between them these days, and
Tommy was relieved to see that they weren't
snapping at each other as much as they had
been. Little by little, they were all getting better,
though Christmas wasn't easy.

They all went to mass together on Christmas
Eve, and John snored softly in the heat of the
small church and the smell of the incense. It
reminded Liz of when Annie had come with
them, and often dozed between them, especially

245

last year, when she was getting sick, and they didn't know it. When they got home, John went right to bed, and Liz finished putting out the presents. It was different this year, for all of them. There was no letter to Santa, no carrots for the reindeer, no delicious pretense, and there would be no wildly excited squeals on Christmas morning. But they had each other.

And as she turned to leave the room, Liz saw Maribeth lumbering down the hall, with her arms full of gifts for them, and she went to help her. She was so awkward now, and definitely slower. She had been uncomfortable for the past few days, the baby was very low, and she was glad that her exams were over. Liz suspected that the baby wouldn't wait much longer.

"Here, let me give you a hand," she said, and helped her put the presents down. It was hard for Maribeth to bend over.

"I can hardly move anymore," she complained good-naturedly, as Liz smiled. "I can't sit down, I can't get up, I can't bend over, I can't see my feet at all."

"It'll all be over soon," Liz said encouragingly, and Maribeth nodded in silence. And then she looked at her. Maribeth had wanted to talk to Liz for days, without Tommy or his father.

"Could I talk to you for a few minutes?" Maribeth asked her.

"Now?" Liz looked surprised. "Sure." They sat down in the living room, near the tree, within arm's length of all of Annie's decorations. Liz felt better about them now. She loved seeing them every day. It was like seeing her, or something she had touched not long ago. It was almost like a visit from Annie.

"I've done a lot of thinking about this," Maribeth said anxiously. "I don't know what you'll think, or say, but . . . I . . . I want to give you my baby." She almost held her breath after she said it.

"You *what?*" Liz stared at her, as though she didn't absorb it. The enormity of what she had just said defied the imagination. "What do you mean?" Liz stared at her. Babies weren't something you gave away to friends, like Christmas gifts.

"I want you and John to adopt it," Maribeth said firmly.

"Why?" Liz was stunned. She had never thought of adopting a baby. Of having one, yes, but not adopting one, and she couldn't even imagine John's reaction. They had talked about it years ago, before Tommy was born. But John never wanted to do it.

"I want to give you the baby, because I love you, and you're wonderful parents," Maribeth said softly. It was the ultimate gift she could give them or her baby. She was still shaking but she sounded calmer. She was completely sure of what she was doing. "I can't take care of a child. I know everyone thinks I'm crazy to give it up, but I know I can't give it what it needs. You can. You would love it and be there for it, and take care of it, just like you've done for Annie and Tommy. Maybe I'll be able to do that too, one day, but I can't now. It wouldn't be fair to either of us, no matter what Tommy says. I want you to have it. I'd never ask for it back, I'd never come back to bother you, if you didn't want me to. . . . I would know how happy the baby was with you, and how good you were to it. That's what I want for my baby." She was crying then, but so was Liz, as she reached for her hands and held them.

"That's not a gift you give to someone, Maribeth. Like a toy or an object. It's a life. Do you understand?" She wanted to be sure she understood what she was doing.

"I know that. I know all of it. It's all I've thought about for the last nine months. Believe me, I know what I'm doing." She sounded as though she did, but Liz was still shocked. And what if she changed her mind? What about her son? How would he feel if they adopted Maribeth's baby, or any baby for that matter? And John? Liz's mind was whirling.

"What about you and Tommy? Are you serious about him?" How could she even know at sixteen? How could she make that kind of decision?

"I am. But I don't want to start off like this. This baby was never right for me. I don't even feel like it was meant for me. I just feel like I was meant to be here for it, for a time, to bring it to the right place and the right people. I'm

248

not the right one. I want to marry Tommy one day, and have children of our own, but not this one. It wouldn't be fair to him, even if he doesn't know that." Liz agreed with her, but it impressed her to hear Maribeth say it. She thought they needed a fresh start one day, if it would ever work for them, and there was no way anyone could know that. But starting at sixteen, with another man's child, was a tall order. "Even if we got married, I wouldn't try to take the baby away from you. It wouldn't even have to know I was its mother." She was pleading with her, begging her to take her child, to give it the love and the life it deserved, and that she knew they could give it. "I feel like it was meant to be your baby, that that's why I came here, because it was meant to be . . . because of what happened . . ." She choked on the words and Liz's eyes filled with tears, "because of Annie."

"I don't know what to say to you, Maribeth," Liz said honestly, as tears streamed down her cheeks. "It's the most beautiful gift that anyone could give me. But I don't know if it's right. You don't just take another woman's baby."

"What if that's what she wants, if it's all she has to give? All I have to give this baby is a future, a life with people who can give it that and love it. It's not fair that you lost your little girl, it's not fair that my baby will have no life, no future, no hope, no home, no money. What do I have to give it? My parents won't let me bring it home. I can't go anywhere. All I can do is work at Jimmy D's for the rest of my life, and I can't even pay for baby-sitters on my salary, if I keep it." She was crying as she looked into Liz's eyes, begging her to take her baby.

"You could stay here," Liz said quietly. "If you have nowhere else to go, you can stay with us. You don't have to give this baby up, Maribeth. I won't make you do that. You don't have to give it up to give it a good life. You can stay with us, like our daughter, if you want, and we'll help you." She didn't want to force this girl to give her baby up, just because she couldn't support it. That seemed wrong to her, and if she took it at all, she wanted to do it because Maribeth really wanted her to, not because she couldn't afford it.

"I *want* to give it to you," Maribeth said again. "I want you to have it. I can't do this, Liz," she said, crying softly, and Liz took her in her arms and held her. "I can't . . . I'm not strong enough . . . I don't know how . . . I can't take care of this baby . . . please . . . help me . . . make it yours . . . no one understands what it's like, knowing you can't, and wanting the right thing for the baby. Please," she looked up at her desperately, and both women were crying.

"You could always come back here anyway, you know. I don't want you to stay away if we do this. No one has to know the baby is yours . . . the baby wouldn't have to know . . . just us. . . . We love you, Maribeth, and we don't want to lose you." And she knew only too well how much she meant to Tommy. She didn't want to spoil anything for him, out of selfishness, or her hunger for another child. It was a rare opportunity, an unthinkable gift, and she needed time to absorb it. "Let me talk to John," she said quietly.

"Please tell him how much I want this," she said, clinging to Liz's hands. "Please . . . I don't want my baby to go to strangers. It would be so wonderful if it were here with you . . . please, Liz . . ."

"We'll see," she said softly, cradling her, trying to comfort her and calm her. She was getting overwrought, begging Liz to adopt her baby.

Liz made her some warm milk after that, and they talked about it some more, and then Liz tucked her into Annie's bed, and kissed her good night and went back to her own bedroom.

She stood still for a long moment, looking at John, wondering what he would say to her, and if the whole idea was more than a little crazy. There was Tommy to think about too, what if he didn't want them to? There were a thousand considerations. But even thinking about it made her heart pound in a way that nothing had for years . . . this was the gift of all time . . . the gift of life that she couldn't bear . . . the gift of another baby.

John stirred slightly as she got into bed next to him, and she almost wished he would wake up so she could ask him, but he didn't. Instead he wound his arms around her, and pulled her

251

closer to him, as he had for years, until tragedy had struck them both numb for the past year. But she lay there in his arms, thinking, about what she felt, and what she wanted, and what was right for all of them. Maribeth had made a powerful argument for them taking it, but it was hard to know if that was the right thing to do, or just very appealing because it was what she wanted.

She lay there for a long time, unable to sleep, and wishing him awake, and finally he opened his eyes and looked at her, as though sensing her anxiousness. He was more than half asleep when he opened his eyes and spoke to her. "Is something wrong?" he whispered in the darkness.

"What would you say if I asked you how you felt about having another baby?" she asked, wide-awake, and wishing that he were more than just semiconscious.

"I'd say you were crazy," he smiled and closed his eyes again, and drifted back to sleep in less than a minute. But that was not the answer she wanted.

She lay there awake next to him all night, and she only slept for a half hour before daybreak. She was too wound up to sleep, too worried, too nervous, too filled with questions and terrors and concerns and longing. And she finally got up, and went to the kitchen in her nightgown and made herself a cup of coffee. She sat there staring into it for a long time, and sipping it, and by eight o'clock she knew what she wanted. She had known it long before, but she hadn't known if she would have the courage to pursue it. But she knew she had to do it now, not just for Maribeth and the child, but for herself, and John, and maybe even for Tommy. The gift had been offered to them, and there was no way she was going to refuse it.

She took her cup of coffee and went back to their bedroom and woke him. He was surprised to see her up. There was no rush to get up this year, no reason to dash into the living room and see what Santa had left under the tree. They could all get up in good time, and Tommy and Maribeth hadn't stirred yet.

"Hi," she said, smiling at him. It was a small shy smile he hadn't seen in a long time, and reminded him of when they had been a lot younger.

"You look like a woman with a mission." He smiled and rolled over on his back, stretching.

"I am. Maribeth and I had a long talk last night," she said, as she approached the bed, and sat down next to him, praying he wouldn't refuse her. There was no way to doctor this up, to delay, or stall. She knew she just had to tell him, and she was terrified to do it. It mattered so much to her. She wanted it so much, and she desperately wanted him to want it, and she was afraid he wouldn't. "She wants us to keep the baby," she said softly.

"All of us?" He looked startled. "Tommy too?

She wants to marry him?" John sat up in bed, looking seriously worried. "I was afraid that would happen."

"No, not all of us. And she doesn't want to marry him, not now in any case. You and I. She wants us to adopt the baby."

"Us? Why?" He looked more than shocked. He looked incoherent.

"Because she thinks we're good people and good parents."

"But what if she changes her mind, and what are we going to do with a baby?" He looked horrified and Liz smiled at him. It had definitely given him a jolt first thing in the morning.

"The same thing we did with the other two. Stay awake all night for two years and long for the days when we got some sleep, and then enjoy the hell out of it for the rest of our lives . . . or theirs," she said sadly, thinking of Annie. "It's a gift, John . . . for a moment, for a year, for as long as life is willing to let us keep it. And I don't want to turn it down. I don't want to give up my dreams again . . . I never thought we'd have another child, and Dr. MacLean says I can't . . . but now this girl has walked into our lives and offered to give us back our dreams."

"What if she wants it back in a few years, when she grows up, and gets married, or even if she marries Tommy?"

"I suppose we can protect ourselves legally, and she says she won't. I don't think she will. I think she really believes that it will be a better life for the baby if she gives it up, and she means it. She knows she can't take care of it. She's begging us to keep it."

"Wait till she sees it," he said cynically. "No woman can carry a baby for nine months and give it up just like that."

"Some can," Liz said matter-of-factly. "I think Maribeth will, not because she doesn't care, but because she cares so much. It's her greatest act of love for that baby, giving it up, giving it to us." Tears filled her eyes and spilled down her cheeks as she looked at her husband. "John, I want it. I want it more than I've ever wanted anything . . . please don't say no . . . please let us do it." He looked at her long and hard while she tried not to tell herself that she would hate him if he didn't let her do it. She couldn't believe that he could possibly know all that she'd been through, and how badly she wanted this child, not to replace Annie, who would never come back to them again, but to move forward, to bring them joy again, and laughter and love, to be a shining little light in their midst. It was all she wanted and she couldn't believe he would ever understand that. She knew that if he didn't let her do it, she would die.

"All right, Liz," he said softly, taking her hands in his own. "It's all right, baby . . . I understand . . ." he said, as tears rolled down her cheeks as she clung to him, realizing how unfair she had been to him. He did know. He was still the same man he had always been, and she loved him more than ever. They'd been through so much and they'd survived. "We'll tell her we'll do it. I think we should speak to Tommy though. He has to feel the same way about it that we do."

She agreed to that, and she could hardly wait for him to wake up. It was another two hours, and he was up before Maribeth. He was stunned when his mother explained what Maribeth had offered them. But he had come to understand recently just how strongly Maribeth felt about giving up the baby, and that she felt it was right for her, and for the baby, and she wanted to do it and give it a better life. And now that he felt he might not lose her after all, he was less pan-icked about forcing her to marry him, and taking on the baby. In fact, he thought it was the ideal solution. He hoped that one day he and Maribeth would have children of their own, but for this child, it was the perfect solution. And he could see in his mother's eyes how much it meant to her. His parents seemed closer already as they talked to him, and his father looked pow-erful and calm, as he sat next to Liz and held her hand. In some ways, it was very exciting. They were about to share a new life.

And when Maribeth got up, they were all wait-ing for her to tell her their decision. They had unanimously agreed to adopt the baby. She looked at them and started to cry in relief, and then she thanked all of them and hugged them, and cried some more. They all cried, it was an emotional time for all of them. A time of hope and love, a time of giving and sharing. A time to start again, with the gift she gave them.

"You're sure?" Tommy asked her that afternoon as they went for a walk, and she nodded, looking absolutely certain. They had opened their gifts and had a huge lunch. This was the first chance they'd had to talk to each other alone since that morning.

"It's what I want," she said, feeling very calm and very strong. She felt more energetic than she had in a long time. And they walked all the way to the skating pond and back, which was several miles. But she said she had never felt better. She felt as though she could do anything now. She felt as though she had done what she had come here to do. She had given them the gift that she was meant to give them. And once she had, all of their lives would be richer from the blessing they had shared with each other.

She tried to explain it to him as they walked back, and he thought he understood it. But sometimes it was hard to listen to her. She was so serious and so intense, and so beautiful it distracted him. When they stopped on the front steps when they got home, he kissed her, and he felt her tense against him as he did, and clutch his hand, and she bent over as he tried to hold her.

"Oh my God! oh my God! . . ." he said, suddenly terrified as he sat her down gently on the step as she held her belly down low and tried to catch her breath in the sharp pain of the contraction. He ran inside to get his mother, and when she came out, Maribeth was sitting there wide-eyed, looking frightened. She was in labor. And it had started harder than she had expected.

"It's all right, it's all right." Liz tried to calm them both and told Tommy to get his father. She wanted to get Maribeth inside and call the doctor. "What did you kids do? Walk to Chicago?"

"Just to the pond and back," Maribeth said, and gasped. She was having another pain again. They were long and hard and she couldn't understand it. It wasn't supposed to start like this, she said to Liz, as she and John helped her inside, and Tommy stood by looking nervous. "I had a stomachache this morning, and it went away after that," she said, unable to believe what was happening. There had been no warning whatsoever.

"Have you had any cramps?" Liz asked gently, "or a backache?" Sometimes it was easy to misinterpret the early signs of labor.

"I had a backache last night, and cramps this morning with the stomachache, but I thought it was from all the food I ate last night."

"You've probably been in labor since last night," Liz said gently, which meant they didn't want to waste time getting her to the hospital. The walk had obviously started her into hard labor. Her due date was the following day, she was right on time, and her baby didn't want to waste a minute. It was almost as though now that she knew the Whittakers were taking it, the baby could come. There was no holding back now.

As soon as they got her inside, Liz started timing her pains, and John went to call the doctor. Tommy sat next to her, holding her hand, and looking miserable for her. He hated to see her in so much pain, but neither of his parents was worried. They were warm and sympathetic to her, and Liz didn't leave her for a minute. The pains were three minutes apart, and they were long and hard, and John came to tell them that Dr. MacLean said to come right away. He would meet them at the hospital in five minutes.

"Do we have to go now?" Maribeth asked, looking very young and very scared, as she glanced from Liz to Tommy to John. "Can't we stay here for a while?" She was almost in tears and Liz assured her that she couldn't put this off any longer. It was time to go now.

Tommy threw some things in a bag for her, and five minutes later they were on their way. Liz and Tommy sat in the backseat with her, and held her between them, and John drove as fast as he could on the icy roads. And as soon as they got to the hospital, Dr. MacLean and a nurse were waiting for her. They put her in a wheelchair and started to roll her away, and she grabbed frantically for Tommy.

"Don't leave me," she begged him, clutching his hands and crying, and Dr. MacLean smiled at them. She was going to be fine. She was young and healthy, and she was well on her way now.

"You'll see Tommy in a little while," the doctor reassured her, "with your baby." But she only started to cry at that, and Tommy kissed her gently.

"I can't go with you, Maribeth. They won't let me. You've got to be brave now. I'll be with you next time," he said, letting go of her gently so they could take her away. But Maribeth turned frightened eyes to Liz and asked her if she would come with her, and the doctor agreed to that. And Liz felt her heart pound as she followed them into the elevator, and then the labor room, where they undressed Maribeth and then examined her to see how far along she was. Maribeth was almost hysterical by then, and the nurse gave her a shot to calm her. She was better after that, though she was in a lot of pain, but once he checked her, the doctor said it wouldn't be long. She was fully dilated and ready to push now.

They rolled her into the delivery room then, and Maribeth clung to Liz's hand, and looked up at her with eyes that trusted her completely. "Promise you won't change your mind . . . you'll take it, won't you, Liz? You'll love it . . . you'll always love my baby . . ."

"I promise," Liz said, overwhelmed by her trust, and the love they shared. "I'll always love it . . . I love you, Maribeth . . . thank you . . ."

she said, and then the pains engulfed the girl again, and the next hours were hard work for her. The baby was turned the wrong way for a time, and they had to use forceps. They put a mask over Maribeth's face and gave her some gas. She was groggy and confused and in agony, but Liz clung to her hand throughout. It was after midnight, when finally a small wail rang out in the delivery room, and the nurse took the ether mask off so Maribeth could see her daughter. She was still half asleep, but she smiled when she saw the small pink face, and then she looked up at Liz with eyes filled with relief and joy.

"You have a little girl," she said to Liz. Even in her drugged state, she had never lost sight of whose baby it was now.

"This is *your* little girl," the doctor corrected, smiling at Maribeth, and then he handed the baby to Liz. Maribeth was much too groggy to hold her, and as Liz looked down into the tiny face, she saw strawberry blond hair, and eyes so full of innocence and love Liz trembled as she held her.

"Hello," she whispered as she held the child that was to be hers, feeling almost as she had when her own were born. She knew this was a moment she would never forget, and she wished she could have shared it with John. It had meant so much to see her born, to see her suddenly emerge and cry out, as though she was calling to them, and telling them she had made it. They had all waited for her for so long. Maribeth was given another shot and she drifted back to sleep, and they let Liz take the baby into the nursery, where they weighed her and cleaned her up. Liz stayed to watch everything as she held the tiny fingers in her hand. A few minutes later, she saw John and Tommy arrive at the nursery window, and both men stood there staring.

The nurse let her hold the baby again and she held it up to John and showed him. And he started to cry the moment he saw their daughter. "Isn't she beautiful?" she mouthed, and suddenly all he could see was his wife, and all they'd been through. It was hard not to think of Annie when she'd been born, but this baby was very different, and she was theirs now.

"I love you," he whispered from the other side, and Liz nodded and mouthed the same back to him. She loved him too, and she realized now with terror and gratitude that they almost hadn't made it. But they had, remarkably, thanks to Maribeth, and the gift she'd given them, and the love they had always shared, but had almost forgotten.

Tommy looked excited when he saw the baby, and he was relieved when Liz joined them so he could ask her how Maribeth was. Liz assured him that she was fine, had been very brave, and was sleeping.

"Was it really awful, Mom?" he asked, worried about her, and impressed by what she'd done. The baby weighed eight pounds fourteen ounces, a big baby for anyone, let alone a sixteen-year-old girl who hadn't known what to expect. Liz had felt sorry for her more than once, but the doctor had been generous with the anesthetics. It would be easier for her the next time. And the rewards for her would be greater.

"It's hard work, Son," Liz said quietly, impressed by everything that had happened. Particularly if you were doing it for someone else, and not keeping the baby.

"Will she be okay?" His eyes asked a thousand questions he didn't completely understand. But his mother reassured him.

"She'll be fine. I promise."

They brought her down to her room an hour later, still half asleep and very woozy, but she saw Tommy instantly and clung to his hand, telling him how much she loved him, and how pretty the baby was. And suddenly as she watched them, Liz felt a wave of terror wash over her like nothing she'd ever known. What if Maribeth changed her mind, if she decided to marry Tommy after all and keep the baby?

"Did you see her?" Maribeth asked Tommy excitedly, as Liz glanced at John and he took her hand in his own to reassure her. He knew what she was thinking, and he had terrors of his own.

"She's beautiful," Tommy said, kissing her, and worried by how pale she looked. She was still more than a little green from the ether. "She looks just like you," he said, but she had strawberry blond hair instead of hair the color of flame.

"I think she looks like your mom." Maribeth smiled at Liz, feeling a bond with her she knew she'd never again feel for anyone. They had shared the birth of her baby. And she knew she couldn't have gotten through it without her.

"What are you going to name her?" Maribeth asked Liz, drifting slowly back to sleep, as Liz felt relief sweep over her again. Maybe she wouldn't change her mind after all. Maybe this really was going to be her baby. It was hard to believe it, even now.

"What do you think of Kate?" Liz asked just as Maribeth closed her eyes again.

"I like it," she whispered, and drifted off to sleep, still holding Tommy's hand. "I love you, Liz . . ." she said, with her eyes closed.

"I love you too, Maribeth," Liz said, kissing her cheek and signaling the others to leave. She had had a difficult night and she needed her sleep. It was three o'clock in the morning. And as they walked softly down the hall, they stopped at the nursery window. And there she lay, all pink and warm and wrapped in a blanket, staring at them, looking straight at Liz as though she had been waiting for her for a long time. It was as though she had been meant for them all along. A gift from a boy who knew none of them, and a girl who had passed through their lives like a rainbow. And as they stood staring at her in wonder, Tommy looked at his parents and smiled. He knew Annie would have loved her.

Chapter Eleven

The next two days were hectic for everyone, and more than a little overwhelming. John and Tommy got out Annie's old bassinet and re-painted it, and Liz stayed up nights draping it in miles of pink gauze and satin ribbons. They got out old things and bought new ones, and in the midst of it all, Tommy went to Annie's grave, and sat there for a long time, looking at the Christmas tree he and Maribeth had brought her and thinking about the baby. He hated the thought of Maribeth leaving them and going home again. Somehow, it had all come so quickly. So much seemed to be happening at once. Much of it was happy. But some of it was painful.

But his mother was happier than he'd seen her all year, and when he saw Maribeth, she was serious and quiet. She'd had a long talk with Liz and John after the baby was born, and they assured her that they would understand if she had changed her mind. But she insisted stead-fastly that she didn't want to. She was sad to give the baby up, but she knew more than ever now, that this was right. The next day, John called his attorney and set the wheels in motion for Maribeth to give up the baby.

The adoption papers were drawn up and

brought to her, the lawyer explained them to her at length, and she signed the papers three days after Kate was born. She waived the waiting period, and signed the papers with a shaking hand, and then she hugged Liz tight, and they asked the nurse not to bring the baby in to her that day. She needed time to mourn her.

Tommy sat with her that night. She was strangely calm about her decision, but wistful too. They both wished everything could have been different. But Maribeth felt that this time she really had no choice. She had done the right thing, especially for the baby.

"It will be different next time, I swear," Tommy said gently, and kissed her. They had been through so much, they both knew it was a bond that would not be severed. But she needed time just to catch her breath, and recover from everything that had happened. The doctor let her leave the hospital on New Year's Day, with the baby, and Tommy came to pick her up with his parents.

Liz carried the baby to the car, and John took pictures. They all spent a quiet afternoon at home, and whenever the baby cried, Liz went to her, and Maribeth tried not to hear her. She didn't want to go to her. She wasn't her mother now. She had to force herself to put distance between them. She knew there would always be a place for her in her heart, but she would never mother her, never be there for her in the dark of night, or with a bad cold, or read her a story.

At best, if their lives stayed entwined, they would be friends, but nothing more. Even now, Liz was already her mother, and Maribeth wasn't.

And as Liz lay holding the baby late at night, watching her sleep, John watched them. "You already love her, don't you?" She nodded happily, unable to believe that he had been willing to let her do this. "There go two years of sleep, I guess."

"It's good for you," she smiled, and he walked across the room to kiss her. The baby had brought them so much closer again. She had given them hope, and reminded them of how sweet life could be when it begins, and how much it meant to share that.

Kate's arrival had brought Tommy and Maribeth closer to each other too. She seemed to need him more than she had before, and all she could think of now was how painful it would be when she left him. She felt strangely vulnerable, and as though she couldn't face the world without him. The idea of going home without him terrified her, and she dragged her feet about calling her parents to tell them the baby had been born. She had been meaning to call them all week, but she just couldn't bring herself to do it. She wasn't ready to go home yet.

"Do you want me to call?" Liz asked two days after they'd come home from the hospital. "I'm not rushing you, but I think your mother would want to know that you're all right. She must be worried."

"Why?" Maribeth said unhappily. She had done a lot of thinking in the last week, and some of it was about her parents. "What difference does it make now, if Daddy hasn't let her talk to me all year? She wasn't here when I needed her. You were," Maribeth said bluntly, and there was no denying the truth of it. She no longer felt what she once had for them, not even her mother. Only Noelle had gone unscathed in Maribeth's heart.

"I don't think your mother can help it," Liz said cautiously, setting the baby down in her bassinet. She had just fed her. "She's not a strong woman." The description of her was more accurate than Liz knew. Maribeth's mother was completely tyrannized by her father. "I'm not sure she even understands how she failed you," Liz said sadly.

"Have you talked to her?" Maribeth asked, looking confused. How could Liz know all that about her? Liz hesitated for a long moment before she answered, and then decided to make a clean breast of it, but Maribeth was startled by what Liz told her.

"John and I went to see them after Thanksgiving. We felt we owed it to you. We didn't even know you'd want to give us the baby then, but I wanted to see what kind of family you're going home to. You're still welcome to stay here if you want, no matter what. I want you to know that. I think they love you, Maribeth. But your father's a very limited man. He really doesn't see why you'd want an education. That was what I wanted to talk to him about. I wanted to be sure he'd let you go to college. You only have a few months until you finish school, and you need to apply now. With a mind like yours, you really owe it to yourself to get an education."

"And what did my father say?" She still couldn't get over the fact that Liz had met them. They'd driven two hundred and fifty miles to see the parents who had rejected her completely for the last six months.

"He said it was good enough for your mother to stay home and take care of her kids, and you could do the same," Liz said honestly. She didn't tell her that he had added "if she can still get a husband now," which he doubted after her indiscretion. "He doesn't seem to understand the difference, or what a rare gem you are." She smiled at the girl who had given her so much. And they wanted to do the same for her. But she and John had already talked about that. "I think he thinks we've filled your head with a lot of wild ideas about going to college. And I hope we have," she said with a smile, "or I'll be very disappointed. In fact," she paused briefly as John walked into the room, "we want to talk to you about something. We had a fund put aside for Annie, when she died, for her education, and we'll need to do the same for Kate now, but we have time for that. We started a college fund for Tommy a long time ago, so we want to give you the money we set aside for Annie, Maribeth, so you know you can go to college. You can come back here, or apply anywhere you want."

Maribeth looked thunderstruck as John continued. "Your father and I discussed it, and we agreed that you'd go back home now, and finish school this spring, and after that, you can pretty much go anywhere. You can come back and stay with us." He glanced at Liz, and she nodded. They had all three already agreed that Maribeth would always tell Kate she was their friend, and not her mother. Maybe one day, when she was grown up, if she needed to know, they would tell her. But in the meantime, Maribeth had no need to tell her the truth, and she didn't want to hurt anyone, not them, or the baby. "You've got your college education now, Maribeth. The rest is up to you. I don't think it's going to be easy at home, your father's not an easy man, but I think he's done some thinking too. He realized you made a mistake. I can't tell you he's forgotten it, but I think he'd like you to come home. Maybe you can all make your peace with each other in the next few months, before you move on to college."

"I hate the thought of going home," she admitted to them, as Tommy joined her and came to sit next to her and held her hand. He hated her going too, and had already promised that he'd visit as often as he could, though it was a good distance. But they both knew six months wasn't forever. It just felt like it to them. But at sixteen, time was endless.

"We're not forcing you to go back," Liz said clearly to her, "but I think you should now for a while, for your mother's sake and to wrap things up in your own mind." And then she said something to her she had promised John she wouldn't. "But I don't think you should stay there. They'll bury you alive if you let them." Maribeth smiled at the accurate description. Being with her parents was like drowning.

"I know they'll try. But they can't do much now, thanks to you." She put her arms around Liz and hugged her, still unable to believe what they were doing for her, but she had done a lot for them too. And as they spoke softly, the baby stirred and woke up, and she started to cry. Maribeth watched as Liz picked her up, and then Tommy took her. They handed her around sometimes like a little doll, everyone loving and cuddling her, and playing with her. It was exactly what she needed, exactly what Maribeth had wanted for her. And watching them, Maribeth knew that Kate would have an enchanted life. It was just what she wanted for her.

Tommy held her for a while and then held her out to Maribeth, and she hesitated for a long moment, and then changed her mind and reached out her arms. The baby instinctively nuzzled her and looked for her breast. Maribeth's breasts were still full of the milk her baby had never taken. And the baby smelled powdery and sweet as Maribeth held her, and then she handed her back to Tommy, feeling over-whelmed by sadness. It was still hard to be so near her. She knew that one day it would be easier, when her own life had moved on. Kate would be bigger then and less familiar than she was now.

"I'll call them tonight," she said about her parents. She knew it was time to go home, at least for now. She needed to make peace with her parents, and then she'd be free to go on, to her own life. But when she called them, nothing had changed. Her father was blunt and unkind and asked her if she'd "gotten rid of it" and "taken care of business."

"I had the baby, Dad," she said coolly. "It's a girl."

"I'm not interested. Did you give it away?" he said sharply, while Maribeth felt everything she'd ever felt for him turn to ashes.

"She's been adopted by friends of mine," she said in a shaking voice, sounding far more grown up than she felt as she squeezed Tommy's hand. She had no secrets from him, and she needed his support more than ever. "I'll be coming home in a few days." But as she said it, she squeezed Tommy's hand again, unable to bear the thought of leaving all of them. It was much too painful. And suddenly going back to her family seemed so wrong. She had to remind her-self it wouldn't be for long. But then her father surprised her.

"Your mother and I will come to pick you

up," he said gruffly, and Maribeth was stunned. Why would they bother? She didn't know that the Whittakers had made a strong case for it. They didn't think she should go home alone on the bus, after giving up her baby. And for once, her mother had stood up to him and begged him to do it. "We'll come next weekend, if that's all right."

"Can Noelle come too?" she asked, looking hopeful.

"We'll see," he said noncommittally.

"Can I speak to Mom?" He said nothing more, but handed the phone over to her, and her mother burst into tears when she heard her daughter's voice. She wanted to know if she was all right, if the delivery had been terrible, and if the baby was pretty, and looked anything like her.

"She's beautiful, Mom," she said, with tears rolling down her cheeks, as Tommy brushed them away with gentle fingers. "She's really pretty." The two women cried for a few minutes and then Noelle got on the phone and sounded starved to hear her. The conversation was a jumble of exclamations and irrelevant bits of information. She had started high school, and she couldn't wait for Maribeth to come home. She was particularly impressed that she was going to be a senior. "Well, you'd better behave. I'm going to be keeping an eye on you," she said through her tears, happy to talk to her again. Maybe Liz was right, and she did need to go back to see them, no matter how difficult it was going to be living in her parents' house again after everything that had happened. She hung up finally, and told Tommy they'd be there the following weekend to take her home.

The next few days went like lightning, as she got on her feet again, and got ready to leave. Liz had taken a leave of absence from work, to take care of the baby, and there seemed to be endless things to do with her, between feeding her and washing her, and doing mountains of laundry. It exhausted Maribeth just to watch her, and it made her realize all the more that she would have been overwhelmed by it.

"I couldn't do it, Liz," she said honestly, amazed by how much work it was.

"You could, if you had to," Liz said to her. "One day you will. You'll have children of your own," she reassured her. "When it's easy and right, with the right husband, at the right time. You'll be ready for it then."

"I wasn't now," she confirmed. Maybe if the baby had been Tommy's, it would have been different. But it would have seemed so odd to hang on to Paul's child, and start out so wrong. She wondered if she ever could have managed it. But she didn't have to think about it now. All she had to do was let go, and leave. That was the hard part. The thought of leaving Tommy was excruciating, and leaving John and Liz was almost as painful, not to mention the baby.

She cried a lot of the time, at almost anything, and Tommy took her out every day after school. They went for long walks, and drove to the lake, and they laughed remembering when he had pushed her in and discovered she was pregnant. They went back to take down Annie's Christmas tree. They went everywhere as though to engrave every moment, every place, every day on their memories forever.

"I'll be back, you know," she promised him, and he looked at her, wishing that he could either move time ahead or back, but away from the agonizing present.

"I'll follow you, if you don't. It's not over, Maribeth. It never will be with us." They both believed that in their souls. Theirs was a love that would bridge the past and the future. All they needed was time to grow up now. "I don't want you to leave," he said, as he looked into her eyes.

"I don't want to leave you either," she whispered. "I'll apply to college here." And other places too. She still wasn't sure what it would be like to be so close to the baby. But she didn't want to lose Tommy either. It was hard to know what the future would hold for them, right now all they knew for certain was what had already come to them, and it was very precious.

"I'll visit," he swore.

"Me too," she said, fighting back tears for the thousandth time.

But the inexorable day was upon them in a

moment. Her parents arrived in a new car her father had been working on in his shop. Noelle was there too, hysterical and fourteen with brand-new braces, and Maribeth cried and held her tight when she saw her. The two sisters clung to each other, relieved that they had found each other again, and in spite of all the things that had changed, to them, nothing seemed different.

The Whittakers invited them to stay for lunch, but her parents said they had to get back, and Margaret stood looking at her daughter with eyes filled with sorrow and regret for all she'd been unable to give her. She hadn't had the courage, and now she was ashamed that someone else had been there.

"You're all right?" she asked cautiously, almost as though she was afraid to touch her.

"I'm fine, Mom." Maribeth looked beautiful, and suddenly much older. She looked more like eighteen than sixteen. She'd grown up. She was no longer a little girl, she was a mother. "How are you?" she asked, and her mother burst into tears, it was an emotional moment, and she asked if she could see the baby. And she cried again when she saw it. She said it looked just like Maribeth when she was a baby.

They loaded Maribeth's things into the car, and she stood there, feeling a rock in her stomach. She went back inside, and into Liz's room and picked up Kate and held her close to her as the baby slept, unaware of what was happening, and that someone important was about to slip out of her life, never to return in exactly the same way again, if ever. Maribeth knew that there were no guarantees in life, only promises and whispers.

"I'm leaving you now," she whispered to the sleeping angel. "Don't ever forget how much I love you," she said, as the baby opened her eyes and stared at her as though she were concentrating on what Maribeth was saying. "I won't be your mommy anymore when I come back here . . . I'm not even your mommy now . . . be a good girl . . . take care of Tommy for me," she said, kissing her, and squeezing her eyes shut. It didn't matter what she had said about not being able to give her anything, or the life she deserved. In her gut, in her heart, this would always be her baby, and she would always love her, and to her very core she understood that. "I'll always love you," she whispered into the soft hair, and then set her down again, looking at her for a last time, knowing that she would never see her that way again, or be as close to her. This was their final moment as mother and daughter. "I love you," she said, and collided with Tommy as she turned away. He had been there, watching her, and crying silently for her sorrow.

"You don't have to give her away," he said through his tears. "I wanted to marry you. I still do."

"So do I. I love you. But it's better this way,

and you know it. It's so good for them . . . we have a whole life ahead of us," she said, clinging to him, holding him, shaking as he held her. "Oh God, how I love you. I love her too, but they deserve some happiness. And what can I do for Kate?"

"You're a wonderful person," he said, holding her with all his strength, wanting to shield her from everything that had happened and hold on to her forever.

"So are you," she said, and then they walked slowly from the room together, and she left her baby behind her. It was almost more than she could do to walk out of the house with him, and Liz and John both cried when they kissed her goodbye, and made her promise to call them, and visit often. She wanted to, but she was still worried it would make them feel that she was crowding into Kate's life. But she needed to see them, and Tommy. Needed them more than they could ever know. And she still wanted a future with Tommy.

"I love you," Tommy said fiercely, like the ultimate affirmation. He knew all her fears, her hesitation about infringing on their lives, but he wasn't going to let her go. And to her, knowing that was a comfort. She knew he would be there for her, if she wanted him, and for now she did. She hoped she always would. But the one thing they had all learned was that the future was uncertain. Nothing they had ever wanted or planned had ever happened as expected. They had never expected Annie to leave them so suddenly or so soon, or Kate to arrive, almost as quickly, or Maribeth to pass through their lives, like a visiting angel. The one thing they knew was they could count on very little.

"I love you all so much," Maribeth said, hugging them again, unable to leave them, and then she felt an unexpectedly gentle hand on her arm. It was her father's.

"Come on, Maribeth, let's go home," he said, with tears in his own eyes. "We missed you." And then he helped her into the car. Maybe he wasn't the ogre she remembered, but just a man with his own weaknesses and tarnished visions. Maybe in some ways, they had all grown up. Maybe it had been time for them to do that.

Tommy and his parents stood watching her as she drove away, hoping she'd come back to them, knowing that if life was kind, she would, to visit, or to stay forever. They were grateful for knowing her, they had given each other precious gifts, of love, and lives, and learning. She had brought them back to life, and they had given her a future.

"I love you," Maribeth whispered as they drove away, and she stared at them through the rear window of her father's car. They watched her wave for as long as she could, and they stood there, thinking of her, remembering, until at last they went back inside to the gift she had left them.

The employees of G.K. Hall hope you have enjoyed this Large Print book. All our Large Print titles are designed for easy reading, and all our books are made to last. Other G.K. Hall books are available at your library, through selected bookstores, or directly from us.

For information about titles, please call:

(800) 257-5157

To share your comments, please write:

Publisher
G.K. Hall & Co.
P.O. Box 159
Thorndike, ME 04986

DEER PARK PUBLIC LIBRARY

3 2244 20007 8729

LARGE TYPE BOOK

STE   Steel, Danielle.

           The gift.

$27.95

DATE			

DEER PARK PUBLIC LIBRARY
44 LAKE AVENUE
DEER PARK, NY 11729

BAKER & TAYLOR

RECEIVED NOV 1 5 1999